SHE
Slipped
AND FELL

SHONDA

authorHOUSE®

AuthorHouse™
1663 Liberty Drive, Suite 200
Bloomington, IN 47403
www.authorhouse.com
Phone: 1-800-839-8640

First published by AuthorHouse 10/8/2008

ISBN: 978-1-4389-0633-1 (sc)

Printed in the United States of America
Bloomington, Indiana

This book is printed on acid-free paper.

It All Starts Here

TINA

Five. It was one of those tummy-churning, excruciating moments. I couldn't lace the seat of the toilet fast enough. The toilet paper only came off the roll a couple of squares at a time! *Four.* My stomach was burning and felt as if it were twisted in numerous knots. I squeezed my butt cheeks together, yet I could tell by the rumbling in my stomach that I only had a few more seconds before my bowels would explode.

Three. It took me several more hurried rips of the toilet paper before I felt that the toilet seat was sufficiently covered. *Two.* I unzipped my denim jeans with the quickness, pulled down my white granny panties, and swiftly sat on the now covered toilet seat. *One.* Splish, splash, relief! I closed my eyes tight as an unbelievable amount of foul, runny boo-boo laced with the beginning traces of my monthly period slithered out of my round, beautiful ass.

The pain in my abdomen momentarily subsided. I could feel a light layer of perspiration on my forehead. I shook my head in disgust as I thought about the pain and suffering women had to go through each and every month all for the sake of menstruation. I never asked to menstruate! Cramps are no joke and it is completely unfair that I have to deal with this foolishness. Eve never should have taken a bite of that stupid apple! I blame her for this monthly madness and she better hope and pray our paths never cross be it in heaven or hell!

Surrounded by the scent of my funk, I decided to reach behind me and do a quick courtesy flush. Hopefully, the flush would help to expedite a speedy riddance of the odor I had let loose. Flush completed, I remained on the toilet unsure as to whether I had any more bowels to release. As I sat there and waited patiently for internal confirmation that I was done, the door to the girls' bathroom was forcefully pushed open. I heard tussling, the shuffling of feet, and the voices of several girls.

"You ain't nothing but a cunt, Kendall Long. When I get through with you, you're going to wish you never laid eyes on Ray-Ray."

"I didn't do anything," I heard a girl, it must have been Kendall, cry. "He approached me. Honest."

"Shut up, bitch! Hold her ass down!"

I'm not sure how many girls were in the bathroom, but it was clear to me that Kendall was solo and she was about to get jumped. I hesitated for a moment. Should I vacate my current position and reveal to Lord knows who that I am the creator of the foul-ass shit smell that was currently overwhelming the bathroom? Should I risk embarrassment in order to help a lonely soul who was about to get her ass whupped for messing with someone's man? Or do I just stay where I am, listen to the beat-down, bask in the scent of my shit, and wait for the girls to leave?

"I'm going to slice your pretty little face, Kendall Long. Hell, I'll be doing you a favor. See, if I cut you up, you won't have to worry about any more boys looking at you 'cause you'll be too damn ugly."

That was enough for me. Cramps and period be damned! I cannot sit here and let this girl get beat down. Even if I don't know her.

I stood up from the toilet that my ass had been having an intense love affair with, wiped several times, quickly searched my purse for a pad which I placed firmly in my underwear, pulled my panties up, pulled my jeans up, fastened them, flushed the toilet, and opened the stall door.

"What's going on, ladies?"

"Hey, Tina," the leader of the pack stammered. "We don't have no beef with you."

"That's good," I replied. "I don't have any beef with you either. Quite honestly, I don't even know who you are. What I do know is that you're threatening to slice up my friend Kendall and I can't let that happen. If you have an issue with my girl, then you have an issue with me. So let's settle it."

Kendall looked at me through teary eyes like I was heaven-sent. I wasn't. I just hated bullies. I was one of, if not *the* most popular girl in Metro High School. I wasn't about to let this apparently timid girl, Kendall, get jumped over a stupid misunderstanding. Granted, I was risking a piece of myself for a girl I didn't know, but I was willing to play the odds and hoped the bullies would leave her alone if they thought she was my friend.

"My bad, Tina," the nameless bully replied. "Ain't nothing going on here. We just wanted to scare your girl, that's all."

"And you did a mighty fine job," I said sarcastically. "See, Kendall's crying. I think that qualifies her as scared. So are we cool here? Do you really want to slice her up or is this over?"

"It's done. We're out." The bully put her knife away and tilted her head at her girls. "Let's roll," she said. The other three girls released Kendall and left.

Kendall lay on the dirty, tiled bathroom floor and stared at the ceiling as countless tears trickled down her unblemished, caramel-colored face.

I went to one of the sinks to wash my hands. After I felt comfortable that my hands were clean, I dampened a paper towel and handed it to Kendall who was still lying on the floor. She took it and wiped her eyes.

"Are you okay?" I asked.

She thought about it before she answered, "I'm fine. Thank you for stepping in."

"It's not a problem," I said as I stared down at her. "I hope someone would do the same thing for me."

"That's funny. You're Tina Jones, right? I don't think there's a soul in this school who'd think about jumping you."

"I think you're wrong, Kendall. My shit stinks just like everybody else's. Didn't you smell it when they pushed you in here?"

"Well, now that you mention it, yes. The funk is definitely poppin' right now!" she laughed.

"Girrrl, you think I don't know? My period just started and I have serious cramps. Normally, I'd wait

SHE *Slipped* AND FELL

till I get home to let my bowels loose like that, but I couldn't hold it." I smiled.

"Do you want some Advil? I just came on yesterday so I know exactly what you're talking about."

"Give me the bottle," I laughed.

And that's how we became best friends.

Friends From Jump - Literally
KENDALL

"Kendall, you are fine as hell." Ray-Ray leaned over from his locker to whisper in my ear.

"Ray-Ray, stop. Don't you have a girl?" I asked hurriedly as I reached for my calculus book and placed it in my backpack.

"Yeah, I got a girl, but she ain't around. Kendall, a man needs constant attention and affection or else he loses interest. So, since my girl ain't showing me no love right now, I ask you, when are you gonna let me melt between your juicy, caramel thighs and rest my head on those big-ass titties?"

"Your head will never rest on these," I said as I boosted my chest with my left hand and closed my locker with my right. As I turned to walk away from Ray-Ray's overactive hormones, I found myself face-to-face with his mean-ass girlfriend, Shay.

"You flirting with my man, Kendall?" Shay asked me.

"No," I said as I tried to push past her.

"Well, why you putting your titties all in his face?" Shay demanded as she grabbed my arm and spun me around.

"Shay, you got it all wrong. Ask Ray-Ray."

Shay turned to Ray-Ray. He had a sheepish, gold-toothed grin on his acne-covered face. I waited patiently for him to repeat his "a man has needs" speech, but all he did was shrug his shoulders.

Shay turned back to me and said, "Bitch, I'm a beat yo ass."

"You and who, Shay? I told you, I don't want your man!"

The next thing I knew, I was pushed towards the girls' bathroom by three unidentified accomplices while Shay walked behind them talking about how bad she was going to jack me up.

As I was forced into the bathroom, a few kids stopped in the hall to see what was going on, but most pretended they didn't even see that I was about to get beat down by four thugged-up chicks. Not a teacher was in sight. It was just another typical day at Metro.

The four girls circled around me and shoved me back and forth. I tried to break out of their vicious ring, but one of them tripped me which caused me to fall. The three flunkies pinned down my arms and legs. I tried to wiggle free, but they had me locked down good. The leader, Shay, pulled a knife out of her bra and opened it.

"I didn't do anything!" I cried. "He approached me. Honest."

Shay said something to me, but between my sobs and my fear, I couldn't hear a word she said. All I could think about was how cold the blade of the knife felt as Shay slid it across my face. I also felt a slight sting as the tip of the knife penetrated my skin and left a tiny hole on my cheek.

Dear God, I've been a good steward of Your word. If a brutal death is Your plan for me, I will humbly succumb to Your will. But if this torture is not Your plan and You desire me to raise up and kick some ass, please give me the strength to do so. Or if I have missed Your calling completely, if you are trying to tell me something, would You please speak a little louder? I need divine intervention right here and right now!

At that moment, I heard a toilet flush and a stall door open. And though I couldn't see her, I knew an angel had been sent to me. *Thank you, Lord! I owe you one big time.*

The Duo

TINA

From the moment I saved Kendall's ass in the bathroom, we became inseparable. How odd considering we are different as night and day. For example, me, Tina Jones: I'm an outspoken, green-eyed, confessed neat freak, community-service-loving shopaholic with two younger siblings. Kendall Long is reserved, somewhat shy, caramel-complected with light brown eyes, dimples, and dark brown hair. Kendall is a soft and stunning spoiled only child, with a love for math, fruit, and computers.

We would have absolutely nothing in common unless we were going to go shopping (my love) for computer software (her hobby) after spending a Saturday morning tutoring kids (me again) in math (that's her) while munching on pineapple chunks, grapes, or kiwifruit. Let's face it, that will never happen!

So what is it that has kept us tighter than a brand new CD wrapped in clear plastic with the adhesive that only hours and hours of peeling and pleading can separate? The short answer is, I don't know. The long answer is, I don't know. The only thing I do know is the likelihood of Kendall and I associating with each other prior to the bathroom situation was slim. For one thing, we didn't run in the same circles. I know for a fact that she wasn't in any of my classes. Plus, Metro is just so doggone big; I can't even recall seeing her face in the crowded hallways.

I tried to bring Kendall around my tight-knit group of friends. Male and female. But this didn't work out like I thought it should. The chicks in my crew greeted her warm enough, I guess, but there was clearly no instantaneous love shared between them and her. Girls can be so damn finicky.

Now the dudes in my clique were really diggin' on Kendall – at first. She laughed and joked with them occasionally, but anytime one of them tried to holla, he got blocked and chopped with the quickness. The male ego can only take so many rejections before it twists reality (no, I'm not interested) into fantasy (even though I just told you no, I really do want to jump into bed with your fine ass), and eventually into aggravated infatuation (that bitch ain't shit). By the last day of school, Kendall had successfully turned all the fellas in my crew into hateful, walking, overloaded sperm bombs.

Before I met Kendall I never had a single friend that was the end-all be-all. I mean, I get along with everybody, but I confide in nobody. That's just the way it is for me. It's safer that way. But when Kendall entered my life, it was like a missing piece to my personal puzzle had been found. The funny thing is that until I met her, I hadn't even known it was lost.

Adieu To Who?

KENDALL

How many people can say their world had changed as a result of meeting someone new? That's exactly what happened to me when Tina rescued me in the bathroom. Now mind you, I could've held my own if the situation was one-on-one with Shay. But the odds decreased significantly when it was four hateful bullies to one innocent me. Tina saved me and afterwards, she wouldn't go away.

Tina waltzed into my life and turned my world upside down. Or maybe she turned it right-side up. It just depends on how you look at it. This girl, Tina, has boundless energy and an ardent boldness that typifies a popular high school student. Combine her cheerful demeanor with her exquisite good looks, pouty lips, and funny-colored eyes and you have a recipe for mystique and charm. She's like a magnet and even though I try to resist the magnetic pull, there really is no escaping it. Everybody at Metro wants to say they're down with Tina Jones. She's got a certain swagger and confidence that makes her friendship a hot commodity. I am honored she chose to be in my corner.

Everything about Tina and the way she lives her life is different from my own. I was brought up in an aging, two-parent, Catholic household. Yes, I said aging. And yes, I said Catholic. Aging because my parents had me unexpectedly and very late in the game. And Catholic because, well, because my parents are Catholic. Not that religion matters or anything. It's just that I don't have any friends, black friends, who were brought up Catholic.

Anyway, the rules of my household are rigid and strict. Having been to Tina's house many times now, I know that her parents allow a tad bit more freedom and flexibility than what I'm accustomed to. Even so, when I invited Tina to my house for the first time, my parents liked her automatically; every structured rule that my parents had ever handed down to me suddenly flew out the window. She hooked them with a wink of the eye, a gorgeous white smile, and kisses to boot. I thought she strictly had the kids at school on lock. I didn't know that shit would work on parents, too! Go figure.

After the bathroom situation, Tina and I hung out on the regular. All the kids noticed and I'm fairly certain they thought I was going to change, ride her jock, and turn into a Tina flunky. That didn't happen, though. Our friendship isn't about me trying to be someone I'm not. I'm still me. I'm still quiet. I'm still the smart but cute girl. Nothing has changed. And I think that's the reason our friendship has endured.

Experimenting
TINA

"Puff, puff, pass. Okay. I got it. I'm a try again," I said as I tried to take yet another puff of the chronic that my boy Eric had purchased a few hours earlier.

We were sitting in his car in an empty parking lot trying to get high before we stepped into a house party. It was me, Kendall, Eric, and Tyson. Tyson, Kendall's date, was already flying high with the birds. Kendall opted to drink some Crown and Coke. Eric was mixing beer and the chronic and still trying to show me how to inhale, but I couldn't do it right. Shit, it burned the back of my throat! Even so, I was determined to find out what all the fuss is about smoking this stuff.

"I don't feel anything, Eric. How do y'all do this shit?"

"Damn, girl, you wasting it! Here. Hold still. I'm a take a puff and blow it into your mouth."

"You're gonna do what?"

"Shut up, girl, and kiss me."

So I closed my eyes, tilted my head to the right, and gently opened my lips as I waited for Eric to put his mouth on mine. When he did, he blew a steady stream of smoke into my mouth, which went directly to the back of my throat. I coughed and sputtered, but Eric didn't take his lips away from mine until all the smoke was gone from his mouth. He took another long drag from the now shriveled joint and repeated the process.

Suddenly I felt a jolt. Or maybe it was a miniature explosion in my head. I felt light. Relaxed. Chill.

So this was it. High. I looked back at Kendall, but she was in a lip-lock with Tyson. I turned and looked at Eric. He smiled at me and I nodded my head.

"Are you there?" he asked.

"Yeah," I said sleepily.

"Cool. You ready to go into the party?"

"Mmm ... Naw ... I just want to sit here for a minute." I rested my head on the back of the seat.

"Baby, I gotta go take a piss. That forty went right through me," Eric replied.

"Okay," I said slowly. "Take Tyson."

"Yo, Ty, man. Quit lip-locking, dawg. I gotta go piss."

Tyson reluctantly pulled away from Kendall. "Man, then go 'head."

"Come on, man."

"Shit. I told you not to drink no damn beer. You shoulda sipped some Crown. I'll be right back, Kendall."

The two guys got out the car and left me and Kendall sitting there.

"Kendall, I don't feel so good," I moaned.

"I don't know why you wanted to smoke that mess, Tina. You don't know what was mixed up in that joint," she said as her hands massaged my shoulders.

My head still rested on the headrest and I closed my eyes as Kendall rubbed my temples, neck, and shoulders. Her fingertips found all the right spots. I felt myself drifting off. I felt like I was flying in a circle, but I was spinning too fast. At this point, Kendall's hands were still rubbing my temples. I reached up with both my hands and grabbed hers with the hope that if I just held on to something, maybe I'd stop spinning. Once I found Kendall's hands, I thought to myself how soft they felt. I vaguely heard Eric and Tyson laughing and opening the car door. Then I passed out.

Schooled on a Sunday
KENDALL

Hangover. I finally know why they call it a hangover. It's 'cause your head hangs over the toilet as you puke your guts out. Then, after you puke, and you attempt to stand, your head hangs over to the side 'cause it's too heavy to hold up the right way. Then, as you slowly crawl to your bed (or the couch), your head hangs over the edge in order to try and restore your equilibrium which is way out of whack.

Hangover. I have one. After Tina passed out, we couldn't go into the party, so Eric drove to the liquor store, flashed his fake I.D. and got some Bacardi and a six-pack of Coke. He then drove us back to the parking lot, opened three Cokes, poured out half the contents of each can, and then replaced the empty space within the can with Bacardi.

I was fine until I drank the Bacardi and Coke. I swear I only took five, maybe six, sips. Suddenly the nice buzz I had turned wicked. I went from giggly to weepy to dizzy to puking to sleep. I'm still not sure how I even made it into my house.

As I opened my eyes, I discovered Tina lying spread-eagle on my floor. She looked dead, but I didn't have time to stop and check as I ran to my bathroom to vomit. My stomach heaved and contracted. The liquid burned as it came up. The brownish liquid gushed out of me and splashed all over the rim of the toilet. I stood. My stomach heaved again. I used to think throwing up chunky food was the absolute worse thing in the world. Now that I've had my first experience puking alcohol, I would like to challenge my original mindset and replace it with the notion that there is nothing, and I do mean nothing, worse than puking smelly-ass liquor.

I stood again and moved slowly over to the sink to wipe my face and wash out my mouth. My head hung to the side as I walked back into my room and collapsed on my bed. Just as soon as my body met the bed, I remembered Tina was last seen lying motionless on my floor.

"Tina," I moaned.

No answer.

"Tina." I said her name a little louder this time.

No answer. Shit. I pushed myself up slowly from the bed. My head was hurting bad. I avoided looking into the sunlight that was making its way into my bedroom. As I walked towards Tina, she coughed, jumped up suddenly, and ran straight to the bathroom.

Well, at least she's not dead, I thought as I listened to the sounds coming from the bathroom. She, too, was puking this morning. I laid back on my bed. I kept my eyes closed and hoped my head would stop pounding. I didn't hear the toilet flush or Tina walk back into my room, but I felt the bed move as she lay down on it next to me.

Neither one of us spoke. I wanted to ask her if her head hurt, but it took way too much effort for me to form the words to make such a long sentence. So, instead, I reached over and grabbed her hand. I squeezed it gently. She squeezed back. We spoke no words as we silently suffered through our hangovers.

Tina and I must have drifted back to sleep because all of a sudden I heard bang, bang, bang. What in the world? I sat up quickly and instantly felt my head swim with nausea.

"Kendall?" my dad said. "Time to get up. We're leaving in thirty minutes."

"Where are we going?" I asked in a muffled, scratchy voice.

"Church!"

"Aww, dad. Not today, okay?"

"Kendall, you and Tina agreed that if we let the two of you stay out late, you would not give us any lip about getting up early to go to church this morning. Your mother and I kept our side of the bargain. It is now morning and we're leaving in thirty minutes. Be ready."

I nudged Tina.

"Hmm," she said.

"We gotta get up."

"Can't."

"Have to."

"Can't."

"My dad …"

"Oh …"

"… said to get up and get ready."

"Can't."

I swung my feet to the side of the bed. My head still hung low and to the side. I hit Tina with my pillow. She slowly rose to a sitting position.

"What do we have to get ready for?" Tina asked.

"Church."

"Oh. I forgot."

Together we stood and made our way to my bathroom. When we stepped through the doorway, it was evident that Tina hadn't flushed the toilet when she had puked earlier. The smell was sour and gut-wrenching. The sight of it goes beyond words. Immediately, we both ran to the commode and puked some more. What a mess!

Somehow, thirty minutes later, Tina and I were showered, dressed, and in the back seat of my parents' car, headed to church. Once there, Tina slept through the entire service. I dozed through most of it, but during one of my waking moments, I heard Father Jean say, "It's written in Leviticus, chapter 18, verse 22: Thou shalt not lie with mankind, as with womankind." I thought to myself, at this point I just want to lie down. Man, woman, be damned. Just give me a freakin' bed.

Boys
TINA

"Eric, you are not getting in my panties. If you want to borrow a pair – fine. But as long as I'm wearing them, you can forget about wearing them with me."

"It's like that?"

"Just like that."

"A'ight then. I'm a have to step and push on."

"Push, brother, push," I said as I hung up the phone.

I looked over at Kendall who was busily typing on my computer and snacking on a banana.

"Girrrl, were you listening to that?"

"Uh-uh. What's up?" Kendall asked as she turned away from the computer.

"Eric is whining 'cause I'm not trying to give the booty up yet."

"I don't know why he's trippin'. He knows he doesn't know what to do with one. Shoot, booties could be on sale at Wal-Mart for fifty cents with step-by-step instructions and I guarantee he still couldn't hit it."

"O-kay!" I laughed as I went over to slap Kendall a high five.

Kendall turned back towards the computer screen. "This guy I'm chatting with right now is spitting out this sob story about how he caught his wife cheating. He wants to meet somebody to ease his pain. P-lease!" she laughed.

"How old is he?"

"I don't know. I'm 'bout to exit this conversation. He doesn't sound right in the head."

"Word," I said. "What do you want to do today? Wanna hit the mall up?"

"What are you shopping for this time?"

"I won't know till I find it," I said, smiling.

Kendall shook her head and rolled her eyes, but she agreed to go. She quickly ended her chat session and then we bounced.

Mama and Dad had bought me a car for my eighteenth birthday. They said it was a birthday/early graduation/better go to college present. Whatever! I had wheels and Kendall and I were rolling to all the hot spots.

As we entered the mall, we quickly noticed how packed it was and realized we picked the right spot to hang out on this particular Saturday afternoon.

Kendall and I turned several male heads as we perused the stores. It was nothing to hear, "Hey, baby" or "Yo, ma, can I get with you?"

I would give the helpless guy a smile and shake my head no. After all, I was shopping. Kendall, on the other hand, flat-out ignored them.

As we shopped, I found two pair of jeans and a smooth-ass Baby Phat shirt all on the clearance rack.

I was too excited. Kendall bought a new pair of Nikes that had just hit the stores.

We left the mall happy and broke. As we were walking to my car, I watched Eric pull in a few spots down from my own. I noticed he had some folks in his car, but I was too far away to identify who was with him.

Kendall and I were trying to decide where to go and eat when Eric, Tyson, and two girls headed toward us.

"Ladies," Eric said.

"Eric," I said, unimpressed.

Tyson kinda stood behind Eric trying to go unnoticed which was totally impossible because he's taller than Eric. Kendall looked at him with murderous eyes.

"Kendall, I can explain."

"Save it, Ty."

"But ..."

"But? But what, Ty? Don't answer that. Just grab the butt of the chick you're with 'cause you'll never caress this one again."

Kendall calmly walked past the foursome. Ty stood there looking stupid. The chick he was with smacked her tongue against the roof of her mouth and rolled her eyes at Kendall. I purposely bumped the chick as I hurried to catch up with Kendall.

"You okay?"

"Girl, yes. I'm just glad I never gave him none," she said as she got in the car.

"That's what I'm talking 'bout!" I hollered. "Make these Negroes wait 'cause once they get it, they don't know how to act."

"O-kay! I'm hungry. Let's go eat."

The After Party
KENDALL

After the break-up that followed my short-lived romance with Tyson, and Tina's dismissal of Eric, it seemed like fellas gravitated to us with full force. Bees to honey. Tina loved the attention. I liked it, too. I mean, what girl doesn't want to feel attractive? Even with all the advances, Tina declined any and all suitors. She said she liked the chase way more than the capture. In other words, flirtation without commitment. So typical.

Tina, Miss Popularity, went to our senior prom solo. That's right. No date. Yet she was the life of the party. Her humanitarian side came out at the prom. She danced and socialized with all the geeks, nerds, and geniuses who didn't have dates. She made their prom night unforgettable. And she made a silent statement to the in-crowd: Everyone deserves to have a good time.

My date, Jaylen, was a twenty-one-year-old, fine, honey-colored brotha that I met online. We had a good time at the prom dancing, talking, and watching folks. After the prom, Jaylen took Tina and me to his apartment. He claimed he needed to change clothes before he took us home. By now, we had all been sipping on a little Courvoisier. Key word equals sipping. Anyway, Tina and I were chillin' in Jaylen's living room listening to a jazz CD, sipping a little of the Courvoisier, and welcoming a slight buzz when Jaylen walked out of his bedroom in some black satin boxers and a freshly oiled, rock hard chest.

I ain't even gonna lie – my panties were instantly wet. I looked over at Tina and noticed she wasn't exactly trying to break her stare from my man.

Jaylen cleared his throat and in a sexy, deep, baritone voice asked, "Can I get you ladies another drink?" He didn't wait for an answer. He smelled like sweet spice as he bent to pick up our glasses and retreat to the kitchen to refill our drinks.

"I … um … better wait outside?" Tina asked.

"No, girl, you stay right here. You are not leaving me alone with him."

Jaylen was back and he set our glasses down in front of us. I wondered if he had slipped one of those date rape pills in our glasses and examined mine closely, but I didn't see anything. Jaylen sat between us. He began to rub my arm.

"I really had a good time tonight, Kendall."

"Me, too."

"Are you interested in taking this night to the next level?" he asked.

"What level might that be?"

"You, me. Let's just see."

"Do you not see my best friend sitting on the other side of you?"

"I see her. If you want, I can call one of my boys to keep her company while we go back to my room."

"I don't think so, Jaylen."

"Oh. Okay. My bad. I just thought ..."

"You thought what? Take a girl to the prom, hit the draws?"

"Well ..." He looked at me sheepishly.

I shook my head from side to side. I noticed that Tina had downed her entire glass of Courvoisier.

"Jaylen, please go put your clothes on," I said to him as I looked at Tina. "It's time to take us home."

"No problem. My bad, Kendall. I just thought, based on your e-mails, that you were ready for a real man." Jaylen rose from the couch with his dick pointing north and protruding a little bit from his boxers. I tried not to look, but I couldn't help myself. He was sexy. And he was a nice guy. This was just a misunderstanding.

"Jaylen, wait." I walked after him. When I reached him, he opened his arms, I walked into them, and he kissed me.

I'd never been tongued so deeply before. He tasted so good. I felt his maleness rubbing against me and for the first time in my life, I considered saying goodbye to my virginity. Jaylen gently caressed my breasts which were straining through my prom dress. I rubbed his penis which had made its entire way out of the slit in his boxers. It was long, thick, and hard. I dropped to my knees to look at it, head-to-head.

Then I remembered Tina and looked over to her. I wasn't surprised to see that Tina was watching us. I curled my right index finger and invited her over. She came. Together we studied Jaylen's manhood. I was the first to touch it. I kinda wrapped my hand around it and moved it up and down. Tina watched me. Jaylen played in our hair.

I quickly became bored with stroking his dick so I stood and kissed his minty-fresh mouth again. Tina still kneeled beside us. Jaylen reached into my prom dress and released one of my breasts. He bent his head and licked it. I motioned for Tina to stand. She did. Jaylen then released one of her breasts and sucked on it. Tina continued to rub him up and down. He turned back to me and found my other breast. He took it, too, into his mouth. I turned my head and stared deeply into Tina's eyes. There was something there, but I couldn't identify the look in her eyes.

Suddenly, Jaylen's body twitched and spasmed a little. I reached down and helped Tina finish him off. He ejaculated strong and steady. His sperm shot right between Tina and me. As he closed his eyes and enjoyed his climax to the very last drop, Tina and I, both bare-breasted, gazed into one another's eyes.

The Closed Door
TINA

The episode at Jaylen's apartment awakened something in me, something that I had been running from for as long as I can remember.

Girly magazines. With naked women. Exposed. Sitting or standing in the most interesting positions. Large and small breasts. Various shapes and sizes. Thin waists. Round asses. Pretty smiles. Alluring eyes.

Pretty. All of the girls were pretty. I discovered the magazines hidden in my dad's nightstand drawer one summer afternoon when I was innocently searching my parents' room for a pad of paper. I was five-years-old.

I remember lying on my parents' bedroom floor flipping through the magazines. I liked what I saw. But even before the magazines, I was always drawn to women. I loved the way they hugged me close. The way they smelled. Their soft bosoms.

As I grew older, I always found myself gravitating toward females. I was friendly with all of them. I didn't know a stranger. Then, as I grew into my teen years, when I was s'pose to be hanging with my girls and looking at guys, I oftentimes found myself studying the girls. Wondering ... Dare I say desiring them? Hell, no. Girls like boys and boys like girls. Girls can't like girls. Right?

College Life
TINA

College life. I loved it. I was on my own doing my own thang. My parents weren't standing over my shoulder questioning me all the time. My brother and sister weren't bugging me. No curfew. No restrictions. I LOVED COLLEGE!

I wished Kendall had decided to attend the same school as me, but she was pursuing an accounting degree with a computer science minor. I was pre-med. Our fields of interest were vastly different. State had a better business school than U so Kendall chose State. U, on the other hand, had a great pre-med program, so I chose U. Thanks to technology, though, we talked daily via e-mail and text messages on our cell phones. It was almost like we weren't even separated. Almost.

Three years into college, the one thing we did that totally conflicted with our friendship was to pledge different sororities. I wasn't sure how it happened; I didn't even know Kendall was going through the pledge process until she showed up at my apartment one weekend wearing the wrong doggone colors!

"Kendall! You didn't even tell me! Ooh, congratulations!"

"You're not the only one who is interested in sorority life," she said to me, referring to the fact that I had crossed the burning sands into sorority land about a month prior to her crossing.

"Clearly," I said. "But I see you went the wrong way," I teased, noting that she was wearing Greek letters that were not the same as mine.

"I went the right way for me. Besides, your colors don't even match!"

"Whateva!" I replied, rolling my eyes all the way to the very back of my head.

"Hater!" she laughed.

"This calls for a celebration!" I said. "I'm a call my sands and invite a few of your sorors over, too. Are you ready to party?"

"You already know! Let's do this."

With that said, Kendall and I went into planning mode as we prepared to have an unsupervised, drinking good time.

She Slipped And Fell
TINA

My two-bedroom apartment right off campus was infamous on the yard for great parties. On this particular Friday night, the music was bumping, the drinks were flowing, the laughter was continuous, and the conversation was filled with put-downs and trash-talking between the rival sororities in the room. Amidst the friendly banter, we had a spades tournament and the two sororities lined around my small living room.

The gathering of women lasted until roughly two in the morning. When the party was over, Kendall and I were left with a huge mess to clean up. Plus, we were drunk. I headed towards the kitchen and Kendall began to tackle the living room. What I didn't know, though, was that someone had spilled gin or vodka (it was clear) on my tiled kitchen floor. So, as I rounded the corner, I slipped and fell smack dead on my ass. The fall must have been loud because Kendall came running to the kitchen from the opposite entrance. She tripped over my foot and landed on top of me.

Being drunk, we both thought it was funny as hell to be sprawled out all over the tiny kitchen floor. But then something happened. I don't know what it was, but Kendall, who was still lying on top of me, brushed a piece of my hair out of my face. I stopped laughing. There wasn't anything blocking my vision and I could see directly into her face and eyes. I thought the alcohol was making me see lust in her eyes because they looked so cloudy and distant. But it wasn't the alcohol. It was real. I shifted myself so that I could sit up; subsequently, Kendall shifted her body which forced me to stay down, beneath her. Then she leaned down and kissed me. She didn't thrust her tongue inside of my mouth or anything. She just sort of nibbled on my bottom lip. When she pulled back, I slowly licked my lips as if I could taste her lips still on mine.

Kendall pushed herself off of me and shook her head. "I'm sorry," she said.

I didn't say anything because I didn't know what to say. Kendall is very attractive. Her skin color reminds me of the caramel candy squares I used to eat when I was a kid. Her face reveals high cheekbones and she has long, dark brown hair that she usually wears in a sleek, wrapped bob. She also has a boyfriend. So do I for that matter. My point is that for the entire time I had known Kendall, I had never seen any indication that she might swing female.

Kendall must have mistaken my silence for anger. She shook her head and began to raise herself up off the floor. At the same time, I was able to sit up from my previously horizontal position. I reached for Kendall to stay seated next to me. We positioned ourselves so that we were both sitting with our backs against the kitchen cabinet. I still didn't say anything and my buzz was fading fast.

Finally, she again said, "Tina, I'm sorry."

I couldn't speak. My mind was whirling. This trick just kissed me. And even though I didn't want to admit it, I liked it. I was trying to weigh the risk. Fact of the matter is, I wanted to kiss her again. Completely. I wanted to explore her body and see if I could figure out the attraction to females that rose up in me from time to time. Yet, Kendall is my friend. My best friend. I don't want to risk our friendship over a kiss.

I stood up and extended my hand for her to take it. She did and I slowly helped her stand. We were almost face-to-face, eye-to-eye. Her eyes were brimming with tears. My eyes were searching hers for understanding. Still, no words. A tear fell from her right eye. I wiped it away and gently caressed her cheek. Then I risked everything I had, our friendship included, as my face descended upon hers; my lips kissed her supple, soft lips. And the wonderment of it all was when she invited my tongue into her mouth to wrestle with her own. Even amidst the alcohol, I could taste a citrus flavor perhaps from an orange she had eaten earlier in the day. Kissing Kendall was sensual and tantalizing. It wasn't hurried or overly forceful. I wanted and needed more. I think Kendall did, too, but we still pulled apart.

"Do you want to do this?" I asked her.

"I've never done anything like this before, Tina."

"Me, neither."

I looked at her light brown eyes a moment longer, then down at her lips. Fuck it. I wanted it. She wanted it. And it was going to happen tonight. I grabbed her hand and led her to my room. We sat down on the bed and kissed again.

My hand timidly wandered beneath her shirt; my thumb rubbed her stomach. I wanted to explore all things female. I slowly unbuttoned her shirt and let it slide down her shoulders. She wore a yellow lace bra. I nuzzled her neck and stroked her cheek before I gazed into her eyes. She lifted my sorority-etched sweatshirt over my head. I unclasped her bra from the front. She unhooked my purple bra from the back. Our breasts were freed as we anxiously wriggled out of our restraints. Her breasts were full. Mine felt ripe and swollen. I didn't want to stop there so I unfastened her pants. She unfastened my black denim jeans. Together we kicked them to the floor. The only thing left was our panties. I was wearing a purple thong. She wore yellow bikinis. Her waist was thin and the panties looked very sexy on her, but they had to come off as my hunger turned to starvation. She slowly pulled down my thong.

And there we were. Naked. Two young college females with everything, and I do mean everything, in proportion. Kendall leaned over me. I could feel the heat radiating from her body. Again we kissed. My hands explored her curves. She was soft in all the right places. She broke free of our kiss and sucked my right breast. I wanted to scream. She sucked my left breast. This time, I did scream as I lay there and let Kendall work her magic. She licked my navel. I shivered and moaned with desire. Then her head was right above my womanhood. I briefly wondered what she was thinking and what she was going to do. I shouldn't have. With a tenderness I had never seen or felt before, she held both of my hands with hers as she kissed it. From top to bottom, Kendall kissed my inverted triangle. She found my clit and gently sucked. It didn't take long for me to explode in her mouth and even though my body shivered, she didn't stop caressing my clit. She kept sucking and licking until I came again. Before this moment, I didn't know I was capable of having multiple, back-to-back orgasms. Yet, with Kendall, I did. And each time I came, it was with more ferocity than the last.

Finally, I gathered the strength to flip her on her backside and I got on top. First, I just sat there and looked at her soft, glistening peanut butter-colored body. I stared at her lips which sparkled from my moisture. I straddled Kendall and began to gyrate slowly. All of my wetness dripped onto her. The combination of our scents, hypnotic, enveloped the room and suggested that desire could not be denied. I continued the circular motion as I leaned down to suck her neck. She gasped and clawed my back. My tongue discovered her ear and tickled the inside. My lips traveled the length of her neck until they found the bare spot right between her breasts. She whispered my name. Acting on instinct, I gently pushed her breasts together and teased her nipples. I had no idea what I was doing. I didn't know Kendall's likes and dislikes. Yet her urging indicated that she liked it all and whatever I decided to do should be done in a hurry.

I scooted down her body and upon seeing her sacred spot, suddenly understood the term "cherry." Kendall's womanhood resembled a succulent, juicy, deep-red cherry, sliced in half with the seed, her clit, inside. A clear juice dripped slowly from within begging for me to bring my willing lips to the brim and take a sip. Nervous, but curious, I slid my hands under her and brought her to my lips. I tilted her just so and tasted a single, sweet drop of juice. That single drop sparked an insatiable thirst within me that encouraged my tongue to plunge deep into her sanctuary. I swirled it and thrust it according to Kendall's rhythm. All the while, I tried to locate her clit with my top lip so that she could experience satisfaction from both angles. I tasted her cum and I wrapped my arms around her waist as she twisted and writhed. When she was done twitching and moaning, I cupped the palm of my hand over her private area and with feathery strokes, brought her to a second climax.

Then we snuggled. She spooned me and rubbed my neck at the same time. Never in all my years had I experienced such a rush. I wanted to do it again. I nudged my bare bottom as deep into Kendall as I could. Her willingness to feed my suppressed appetite was one that I had never before experienced. We kissed, we rubbed, we squeezed, we licked, we sucked, and we came several times during those wee morning hours.

At one point during our sexual exploration, Kendall got up and grabbed a bottle of white wine from the kitchen. She proceeded to pour it all over me from my neck to my navel. Then she licked and sucked it off with the utmost care. Before we knew it, it was six o'clock in the morning. Together, we witnessed the sun rise.

"Tina?"

"Hmm?"

"I've never done anything like that before."

"Are you sure?" I asked.

"Positive."

"Well, I haven't either," I responded. "Did you enjoy it?"

"Do you even have to ask?"

"What now?"

There was silence before Kendall replied, "Let's do it again."

"What about Marcus and Tonio?" I asked, referring to our boyfriends.

"I don't know, Tina." Her response was solemn.

We were quiet for a few minutes before I asked, "Kendall, had you thought about me before tonight?"

"Yes."

I smiled because I didn't want our lovemaking to be the product of a drunken rendezvous even though I'd venture to say we were both very sober during this experience.

Suddenly the need for sleep overwhelmed me. "Kendall."

"Yes?"

"I don't want tonight to ruin our friendship."

"It won't. We'll always be friends. Now go to sleep."

I let her hold me tight as we fell into a deep sleep. I didn't wake up again until late Saturday afternoon. I opened my eyes and I felt Kendall behind me, still holding me tight. The night before wasn't a dream. I had my first sexual experience with a beautiful woman who also happened to be my very best friend and I loved it. I pushed myself closer to Kendall and just lay there replaying the evening and subsequent lovemaking in my head.

Kendall had never flirted with me before. Over the years, we have shared a lot of firsts together, but nothing compared to this, not even the episode on our prom night with Jaylen. Kendall never said anything to me about having a curiosity about women. All this time I thought I was the only one. Whenever Kendall came to U for a weekend, she'd stay in my spare room or at her boyfriend's place. The guys on campus would try to holler at her on the down low, but she was devoted to Marcus.

As for me, I was well-known on the yard and often described as "fine as hell!" With my long, jet-black hair, natural green eyes, and milk-chocolate complexion, I was a prize. Believe that. Plus, I worked out five days a week and had the abs and ass to prove it. Fellas tried to holler all the time, but I was Tonio Thompson's girl. Tonio was a senior and the star quarterback of U's football team.

So my point is, it's not like we were two manly-looking or ugly-ass females. We weren't. Make-up, skirts, heels… You name it – we were as feminine as they come. On the outside, we appeared as regular as anybody else. But the experience last night proved that Kendall and I were clearly a different breed.

Just then, someone banged on the door. Judging by the fierceness of the banging, it could only be Marcus or Tonio. Kendall was in a deep sleep and didn't appear to hear the pounding, so I untangled myself from her clutches, threw on my slippers and robe, and went to answer the door. As I suspected, Tonio was on the other side.

SHE *Slipped* AND FELL

"Hey, baby! What are you doing still in your pajamas?" He peeked inside my robe and raised his eyebrows when he saw that I was naked beneath it.

"I drank too much at the party last night and slept in. I was just about to get in the shower when you knocked so I had to throw my robe on." I was already lying to my man.

"Can I join you?" Tonio asked as he grabbed at my robe.

I swatted his hand. "I don't think so," I said as I backed away from him. I glanced around and realized Kendall and I never did get around to cleaning up the apartment. "Look at this mess. Maybe I'll clean up first," I said as I passed by the kitchen and stared at the spot where Kendall and I shared our first kiss the night before.

"Y'all must have had it going on in here! Sorry I couldn't make it. The fellas and I went to the bar and drank quarter drafts."

"That's okay. It was really just the girls anyway," I replied, thinking that if he had been there, Kendall and I would not have hooked up last night.

"Where's Kendall? Is she going to help you clean up this mess?" Tonio asked as he watched me pick up paper cups and toss them into the trash.

"She's still asleep."

Tonio walked up slowly behind me and grabbed my breasts. "Let's do it quietly in here. She won't hear a thing." He nibbled my ear.

Again I pushed him away. "Quit playing, Tonio."
"Who's playing?"
"You. If you want to do something, help me clean up."

Tonio looked around and suddenly remembered what he came over for. "Aw, baby, you know I would, but I actually stopped by to get my econ book. I think I left it here Thursday night when we were studying." He walked towards my room.

"Wait!" I shouted because I didn't want him to walk into my room and see Kendall naked and asleep in my bed.

"What's up?"

"I'll get your book."

"I'll get it. Go ahead and clean up."

"Tonio! You can't go in my room."

"Why?"

I paused, "Kendall's asleep in there."

"Why is Kendall sleeping in your room?"

I had to think fast. "She was so drunk last night that she went to bed before the party was even over. I guess she threw up in her bed and got up and went to my bed. When the party was over, I went to her room to check on her and saw the puke on her sheets, but Kendall wasn't there. I checked the bathroom, no Kendall. I went to my room and there she was passed out on my bed. So I left her alone and slept on the couch." Lie number two.

"Dang, she must have gotten fucked up."

"Yeah. Linda made the margaritas last night."

"Linda the blenda ... That girl knows she can hook up the drinks!"

"Yeah. Wait here. I'll go get your book."

"Bet." Tonio sat down on the couch and turned the television on.

I went to my room and was surprised to see Kendall sitting up on the side of the bed with the sheet wrapped around her. She watched me enter my room. She must have heard me lie to Tonio. She didn't say anything, she just watched me. Even with the blinds closed I could see the passion marks I had placed all over Kendall's neck the night before. I found Tonio's book on my desk. I picked it up, went to Kendall, gently stroked her hair, and then left the room to take Tonio his book.

"Thanks, baby. What do you want to do tonight?"

"First, I need to clean this place up. Then I'm going to take a long, hot shower. Then I'm going to eat and sit on the couch in front of the tv."

"Well, I'll catch up with you later." He stood up from the couch and headed to the door. I followed him. When he reached the door, he turned around and bent down to give me a kiss. I turned my head so that he'd kiss my cheek.

"What's that all about?"

"I haven't brushed my teeth yet." Lie number two and a half. After all, I hadn't brushed my teeth. But I didn't want him to kiss me either.

Tonio looked at me as if to say so what. I didn't meet his eyes. Instead, I stared at the tiny mole above the left corner of his lip. He shrugged, opened the door and left. I closed the door behind him and leaned against it. Almost three lies in less than thirty minutes. What the fuck?

I slowly walked to my room. I was scared. What if Kendall regretted last night? What if she despised me? Us?

When I reached my room, she was lying down again, under the covers, staring at the ceiling. She was clearly in deep thought.

"I'm sorry you had to lie to Tonio."

"How much did you hear?"

"Everything."

"Oh. Well, you weren't standing out there with a gun to my head making me tell those lies."

"No, but I was in your bed last night changing both of our lives forever."

"It was a mutual decision, Kendall."

"I kissed you first," she said.

"I'm glad you did," I said as I got in my bed and lay down beside her. We turned so that we were facing each other.

"Does this make us gay?"

"I don't know. I don't think so."

"I am not gay, Tina."

"Okay."

"So now what?" she asked.

"I'm not sure."

The Aftermath
TINA

During the days following our night of discovery and passion, Kendall and I decided that she should transfer to U for the summer. It was an easy decision and it made a lot of sense. I had an extra bedroom that was hers when she came down for the weekends anyway. Her boyfriend already attended U. Plus we'd get to spend more time together.

Once she arrived for summer school, we tried our damnedest to act like nothing had happened between us. But the fact of the matter was something had happened. We became more sensitive to each other. It seemed like whenever we were together, we found ourselves bumping into each other unnecessarily or finding some reason to touch the other.

In public, we were friends and purposely avoided the appearance of being too close. Yet when on the yard, we always observed what the other was doing and who she was doing it with. The hardest part was seeing the other with her boyfriend. I hated Marcus every time he stepped foot in my apartment. I'm sure Kendall felt the same way about Tonio.

One sunny afternoon on the yard, a bunch of my sorors and a few members of the football team were standing around talking between classes when Tonio suddenly bent down to kiss me. As his lips unexpectantly met mine, I saw Kendall walk by out of the corner of my eye. I watched her as Tonio kissed me. I saw her face tighten then look sad. I felt my heart twisting. The result was a lifeless kiss for Tonio.

At home, behind closed doors, we snuggled as we watched television. We had candlelight dinners. We tickled each other. We slept together whenever our boyfriends weren't over, which we seemed to discourage more and more. Yet, we never kissed and we did not have sex again. Every time I saw her suck the juice from one of the many pieces of fruit she liked to snack on, I prayed that just once I could turn into the fruity flesh or even the seed just so I could feel her lips engulf every inch of me.

As I sat in my room studying, I kept getting distracted by thoughts of Kendall who happened to be in her room studying. It had been weeks since our first encounter. Things were tense when we were in public or with our respective boyfriends. I was living a secret life and it was driving me crazy.

I closed my book and got up to go to Kendall's room. I watched her from her doorway. She was sitting at her desk and her head was bent over her book as she wrote something down. As I stared at the back of her head something came over me. It was a feeling so strong that I was surprised by its intensity. I just wanted to wrap my arms around her and protect her.

Forever. Now why the hell I thought I could protect somebody was beyond me. Is that the way a guy feels when he really cares for a girl? Was I turning into a guy? I reached up to see if I had suddenly grown a beard. I was relieved to find that my face was as smooth as ever. I must be losing my mind. I'm not a guy. I don't want to be a guy. I have no desire to try to think or act like a guy. I am a female. Period.

Kendall must have felt my presence because she looked up from her book and turned towards me.

"What's wrong, Tina?"

"Nothing."

"You sure?"

"No," I said as I walked into her room and sat on her bed. She got up from her desk and came to her bed to sit beside me. "My parents would kill me if they found out I was here messing around with a female."

"So would mine. I can hear my mama now: The Bible says men are not supposed to sleep with men and women are not supposed to sleep with women."

"Kendall, despite what my parents would do, think, or say, I don't like living this double life. I don't like only being able to touch you within the confines of our own home. I don't like watching you with Marcus. And I damn sure don't like it when he spends the night here or you there," I said.

"Well, how do you think it makes me feel to see you on campus kissing Tonio? Or how do you think it makes me feel to hear him say 'baby this' and 'baby that'?" she responded. "Don't you realize that I want you all to myself? Don't you think that I wish we could stay in here all of the time and never have to open our front door?

"I never in my wildest dreams would have thought that one night, one experience, could turn my whole life upside down. I wouldn't give that night back for anything in this world," Kendall cried.

"So what do we do, Kendall? We can't keep living like this. We can't keep pretending that everything is normal."

"Can you commit to me, Tina? Can you hold my hand in public? Can you kiss me on the yard in front of our sorors and friends and all the other people out there? Can you slow dance and grind with me at a party instead of watching me dance with my boyfriend out of the corner of your eye?" Kendall asked.

"I want to."

"But *can* you?"

"I don't know. Maybe ..."

"You can't, Tina. And neither can I. I'm not strong enough to defy society and flaunt a girlfriend. I'm not strong enough to face my parents. I'm not strong enough to challenge God whom I worship."

"So we should stop this madness and go back to being who we were before that night? It sounds so ridiculously simple, but it's not. At least, not for me. Do you realize that our night together is subconsciously making me confront some issues that I would have preferred to keep hidden? Did you know that I've always thought there was something unusual about myself? I've had crushes on girls before, Kendall, but I've never acted on them.

"That night with you was twenty-one years of pent-up confusion. And now that I've explored, I'm even more confused. It seems as if I have lost my virginity twice. Once to a man – Tonio. And once to a woman – you. I liked it both times. But to be honest, Kendall, I liked it more with you. Yet society says that I can't be with you. It's not fair."

Kendall pulled me towards her for a hug. I melted deep down inside her arms. Her dark caramel skin was warm and I imagined it to taste like a sweet caramel apple. My head rested on her shoulder as she gently stroked my hair.

Though she wasn't staring at my eyes she said, "You have the prettiest damn eyes, Tina Jones. When we first met on the floor of Metro's bathroom, I wondered if your eyes were real, but it was way too soon for me to ask you. Then, one afternoon, the sun hit your eyes just right and they looked like emeralds. It was then that I knew they were real. Sometimes they look hazel. Sometimes they look green. How is that possible? Long, well-kept hair, milk-chocolate skin with a tight-ass body, a gorgeous smile, and lips designed for sucking. Girl, you have it going on. I've always been proud to call you my friend. I've always been satisfied with having you strictly as a friend. I never once entertained the thought of us being something more. But I will admit that I've always been attracted to you. I love you. Your personality. Your spirit. I never meant to slip and fall. Let alone on top of you! I never meant to kiss your beautiful, soft lips." Kendall stopped stroking my hair. She pushed me out of her arms and made me look at her as she spoke. "I never meant to fall in love with you, Tina."

I looked at Kendall in disbelief. "How can you love two people?"

"I don't love Marcus. I've never confessed my love for him," she said. "What about you? Do you love Tonio?"

"Yes. Or at least, I thought I did. But if I truly loved him, I never would have slept with you."

"Do you love me?"

I hesitated, but only for a moment, "Yes."

"Are you in love with me? Tina, loving someone and being in love are two different things."

I recalled the overwhelming need to protect Kendall I had experienced only moments before while standing in her doorway and silently watching her study. I remembered the intense jealousy that overcame me whenever Marcus set foot in our apartment lately. And then I imagined life without her. I replied softly, "Yes, I'm in love with you."

Kendall smiled and I finally got the opportunity to kiss her amazingly soft, full lips again. I pulled away. "I can't commit to you in front of the outside world. I don't know how to do that yet, Kendall. But I need to stress the word 'yet'. For now, behind closed doors, I promise to fulfill all of your dreams and to comfort you when you need comforting. And I'll do my best not to hurt you. I'm already your friend. I'm your sister in spirit. Now I want the opportunity to be your full-time lover."

"Okay, but I'm not going to be your bitch!" Kendall broke up some of the tension in the room with her crazy sense of humor. We both burst out laughing. Her dimples sunk deep into her cheeks causing my heart to race and my stomach to flutter.

"What? Somebody's got to wear the pants around here. It might as well be me!" I laughed.

"Naw, girl. There'll be no role-playing up in this joint. You keep being you and I'm going to keep being me." Then she got serious as she said, "Besides, I like it when you wear skirts and show off those long-ass legs."

"Oh you do, do you?"

"Mmm hmm." Kendall's voice got husky.

"You like these long-ass legs right here?" I asked as I wrapped my legs around her.

"Yeah. Those are the ones." She slowly rubbed my thighs through my jeans.

"What else do you like?" I asked seductively.

"You."

"Prove it," I said.

And she did. That night, this time in her room and on her bed, Kendall proved to me that the decision we had just made was the right one.

Breaking Up is Hard to Do
TINA

With a clear understanding of what we wanted from one another, we decided it was time to give the fellas the boot. Kendall successfully ended her relationship with Marcus. Breaking up with Tonio, however, proved to be far more difficult.

"What do you mean, you want to end the relationship?"

"Well, you're graduating and possibly going pro. I don't want to interfere with that. I have another year left. It just makes sense."

"No, it doesn't just make sense, Tina! I love you, girl! We've been together for three years! You don't just throw three years away.

"Are you worried that I won't be faithful? I've been one hundred percent faithful to you here and you know how many girls come knocking on my door! I don't want those girls. I like what I have with you."

"But, Tonio, you'll be so busy with training camps. And how will we handle the distance thing?"

"Baby, I'll be making enough money to fly you to me whenever you want. And the off-season can be our time."

"I don't know, Tonio."

"Who is it, Tina?"

"What?"

"Who is it?"

"Nobody."

"Then why are you kicking me to the curb out of the blue? Baby, I thought you loved me."

"I do love you. I just," I paused, "I'm just not in love with you. It's all happening too fast. I've been with you my entire college career. I need an opportunity to explore and breathe a little. I don't know how I can make you understand."

Tonio sat on the couch for a minute. He looked as if I had run over him with a truck. I'd never seen a two-hundred-and-fifty-pound man cry. But cry he did.

"Tina, I love you. I love you enough to let you go and see what it is you think you're missing. But you can't come running back to me if you don't find whatever it is you're looking for. And I can't promise that I'll wait for you either. We have a good thing baby. Are you sure you want to let it go?"

I put my head in my hands. I was crying, too. Despite how I felt about Kendall, I cared a lot for Tonio. He had been my big teddy bear for three great years. But by not knowing who I truly was and what I truly wanted, I was only hurting him. I didn't want to hurt Tonio any more than I wanted to hurt Kendall. I had to make a choice because cheating was not my thing. Besides, I needed to find out which way I truly swung. Was it male or was it female? I could honestly say that I liked them both, but right now, Kendall's soft lips, long hair, pretty smile, and tender touch were beating out Tonio's strong frame and gentle heart.

"I have to let you go, Tonio." With that, he got up and walked out of my life.

We had each broken up with our boyfriends on a Friday afternoon. We lay in each others arms on Friday night. And then, on Saturday morning, we drove home to spend the weekend with our families.

Dad was heartbroken when he found out I broke up with Tonio. "What do you mean, y'all broke up? Tina, the boy is headed to the pros. He's going to make hundreds of thousands, if not millions, of dollars! Have you lost your damn mind?"

"Daddy, it's not about the money."

"The hell it ain't!"

"Daddy, listen. I've spent the past three years of my life with Tonio. So basically, I left your house and guidance and went right into the arms and protection of Tonio. I haven't had the chance to be with anybody else or to see what life has to offer."

"Well, little girl, I'll tell you what life has to offer. Bills, bills, and more damn bills! Now I can understand you wanting a little space, but you would have had that anyway because Tonio isn't going to be on campus anymore. You would have had all the space that you could possibly need."

"Daddy, I can't make you understand."

"Clearly," he said as he stormed out of the house.

I walked into the kitchen where Mama and my sister, Kim, were sitting.

"Tina, Tonio is fine! I'm gonna have to agree with Daddy on this one. And Ryan was looking forward to getting free tickets to the games," Kim said, referring to our brother.

I shook my head and walked to my childhood bedroom. Mama followed me.

"Tina, I don't know what's going on in your life right now, but I suspect there's more to it than what you're telling us. I see something in those crazy green eyes of yours. Do you want to talk about it?"

"Mama, I can't. Not right now. Not until I have it all figured out."

"Honey, if you need me, you know where and how to find me. And don't worry about your father, he's not thinking straight right now. He only sees lost revenue."

As Mama walked out of my room, I lay across the bed and thought to myself there was no way in hell I could tell her that I had fallen in love with a beautiful caramel candy named Kendall.

I reached over, picked up the phone, and dialed Kendall's home phone number.

"Hello."

"Hi, Mrs. Long. May I speak to Kendall?"

"Just a moment." There was silence as I waited for Kendall to come to the phone.

"Hello," Kendall said.

"Hey, girl. It's me, Tina. I just called to tell you that I'm going to head back to school tonight. I don't think I can stay home for the entire weekend."

"What happened?"

"I can't really talk about it. Do you think your folks can drive you back tomorrow?"

"Of course they can, but ..." she paused. "Tina, I'll ride back with you. You sound like you need a friend. That's where I fit in, no questions asked."

"Okay. I'll pick you up in a few."

Trying to Look Normal
TINA

Back at school, Kendall and I settled back into the school grind. I worked mornings, studied, and then attended class in the afternoon. Kendall, never the early riser, tended to sleep till noon, go to class right after lunch, and then on to work.

Kendall would study for a few hours each evening and I would usually go work out at the gym while she hit the books. We slept together every night. Since Kendall was a confessed yet non-recovering slob, we usually spent our sleeping and sexual exploration hours in my room because her bed was typically covered with clothes and other miscellaneous items.

Kendall and I had a good routine and we managed to keep our friendship in check. We argued from time to time just like we did – and over the same things – before we became lovers. For example, I'd get mad at her when she'd leave half-eaten plates of food on the counter instead of throwing the food away and washing the plate. My pet peeve was that she rarely ever cleaned the bathroom. The girl truly was trifling in my book. And she had the nerve to get mad at me for leaving lights on all over the apartment. She was straight-up on the tight-wad tip when it came to paying bills. What she didn't seem to understand was that I left the lights on so she could see how filthy the place was when she didn't clean up after herself.

We each found time to hang out with our sorors and to party. It always sent tingles up my spine when one of the sororities or frats threw a party because the ladies typically dressed sexy as hell. It was a competition between the sororities to see who would wear what and who would look the sexiest. Kendall and I had no problem competing. At these parties I'd tend to wear clothing that exposed ample thighs or tops that exposed large amounts of breast or my flat stomach with the diamond belly-piercing.

I would watch my girl do her thang on the dance floor and lick my lips knowing that I'd be the one between the sheets with her later. Or I'd check out the fellas eyeing her, drooling for her, or trying to holla at her and just chuckle to myself 'cause quite frankly, they couldn't have her. Sometimes I'd catch Kendall on the side of the dance floor presumably talking with her sorors, but actually watching my every move. Her eyes would secretly devour me with a masked hunger that only I could recognize. And as I watched her watching me, I'd remember her lying on top of me that first night in our apartment and I'd recall the desire that she couldn't hide. Then I'd swallow her with my green eyes and silently nod to let her know that I am all hers.

To keep everything as normal as possible, we always caught a few dances with a couple of dudes.

But it always worked out where even though we were dancing with someone else, we could always see the other. So regardless of who I was dancing with, I could always look over his shoulder and see Kendall. And she would undoubtedly be watching me.

Now I'm not saying that this was the easiest thing in the world to achieve. In fact, it was hard as hell. Not the physical act of searching for Kendall – that was easy. But watching her dance with a dude who had probably had a few too many drinks and Lord knows what else prior to the party – that was hard. There were a couple of times when I'd have to endure watching some brotha who couldn't seem to keep his hands off my woman as they danced. Sometimes the brotha would whisper something in her ear and I'd watch her laugh and it really, really pissed me off. Yet nothing would compare to the time when a brotha was trying to rub my booty and Kendall jumped out of the dance line with her sorors, yanked my ass off the dance floor, and damn near cussed me out on the spot. I had to remind her where we were and that people were watching. She managed to regain her composure, but not before several onlookers observed the incident. After that particular party, Kendall did not speak to me during the entire ride home.

"Kendall, why are you trippin'? It was a dance. You know a brotha is going to try and cop a feel."

Silence.

"Kendall, dammit, how many times have I had to stand back and watch some dude whisper in your ear or try to nibble on your neck? How many fuckin' times? But we both agreed that it's the nature of the

57

beast and we'd just have to deal with it. Why, then, are you trippin' on me?"

By this time, we were home. As Kendall put her key in the lock, she didn't say anything. She pushed the door open and let me walk in. As she closed the door she said, "So I guess you haven't heard?"

"Haven't heard what?" I asked.

"TJ has a thing for you. His frat told me now that Tonio is out of the picture, TJ's gonna make a move on you."

"Is that right?"

"Yeah."

"Let me get this straight. You're mad at me 'cause TJ has a jones for me. A jones, which I might add, I knew absolutely nothing about until now. And since TJ was trying to get his grip on at the party, you get mad at me?" My voice rose an octave after each sentence.

Kendall didn't say anything.

"Let me ask you something, Kendall. Do you think any of those brothas that you dance with might like you?"

She still didn't say anything.

"I can't control how TJ or any other brotha out there might feel about me. Nor can you. We are both two very attractive women. Fellas are going to step to us – they always have. Think back to high school. Remember how we'd go to the mall and fellas would try to approach us? Nothing has changed! They definitely aren't going to stop now that they think we are single."

"I know."

"So again I ask you, why are you trippin'?"

"Tina, look, I lost it. Okay? Jealousy got the best of me tonight. Simple and sweet: Jealousy."

"Why? You know I don't want them."

"But the fact that they want you pisses me off. It's disrespectful," she said with a pout as she kicked off her shoe.

"How is it disrespectful when they don't know about us?"

"Tina, I don't know. It just is. Damn," she said as her pantyhose tore.

"Come here, girl. Calm down." I unzipped the back of her dress so she could take it off.

Kendall let it drop to the ground and I admired her ass which was scantly clad in black lace panties.

"Another thing, Tina. Maybe you should show less skin when we go out."

My mind quickly registered the message Kendall just delivered to me. "Now hold the fuck up. If you're asking me to change who I am in order to help you overcome your insecurities, you can kiss my ass. You know good and damn well that my body is my temple and if I choose to expose it or flaunt it, that's my business. You know what, I can't even have this conversation with you right now. Good night." I stomped out of her room and into mine where I slammed the door. I couldn't believe that my girl had the nerve to trip like that.

"Tina, can I come in?" Kendall asked from outside my door.

"Hell naw. Leave me the fuck alone," I replied. She opened the door anyway and as she walked in I noticed that she had put her robe on.

"I'm sorry. I was out of line."

"No, what you were was out of your damn mind. What's wrong with you?"

"I don't know."

"Don't go getting all insecure on me, Kendall. I can't deal with that shit."

"I'm sorry," she said as she walked towards me.

"Don't think you're about to waltz over here and try to make up with me. I'm not feeling you right now."

Tina continued to walk towards me. She circled around me and finally settled behind me where she lifted my hair and kissed the back of my neck. "I'm sorry," she said again.

"Dammit, Kendall, I said stop." But she continued to kiss the back of my neck knowing that it was my one weak spot. "Stop," I said unconvincingly.

"I'm sorry," she said again as she turned me around and kissed my exposed cleavage.

"Kendall, do you realize this is our first relationship fight? I don't want to gloss over it by having sex."

"Me, neither," she said as she untied my halter top. She held it closed, though, as she said, "What I'm trying to do is make love to you like I've wanted to do all night. I wanted you as I watched you on the dance floor. I wanted to grab your booty when TJ did it. Okay? Is that what you want to hear?" Kendall paused, but she still held my top closed. "Baby girl, I just want to make love to you." She let the strings of my shirt fall. When she did, my breasts were totally exposed. I pulled my shirt back up.

"On one condition," I said.

"What?"

"Don't do this again, Kendall. Don't repeat tonight. I don't like this side of you. Jealousy is not you. Your actions almost brought attention to our situation tonight. And unless you're ready to share our relationship with the world, you need to check yourself."

"Consider me checked."

"Consider me yours," I replied as I let my shirt fall.

Confrontation

TINA

The rest of the semester sped by almost flawlessly. To avoid unnecessary arguments, Kendall and I went out less often. This, however, sparked displeasure from both of our respective sororities.

"Tina, where have you been?" asked my sands Tranay.

"Working."

"How come we don't see you out anymore?"

"Girl, I'm usually too tired or studying."

"Even on Saturday?" asked Tranay.

"Yeah, even on Saturday."

"What are you and Kendall hiding up in that joint? She's about as incognito as you are."

"We aren't hiding anything. We're trying to get through our senior year. We're trying to get our minds right for the future."

"Whatever, sands."

"What are you saying?" I asked.

"I'm saying we're seniors! We got it made now! There's a party going on damn near every other night.

And you and Kendall don't come out of the house except to go to work or class."

"That's not true. I work out every night."

"Tina!"

"What? I just don't feel like going out that's all."

"Whatever."

Around the same time, Kendall and her sorority sister, Linda, had a similar conversation while studying at the kitchen table.

"Kendall, can I ask you something?"

"Sure, soror, what's up?"

"What's up with you and Tina?"

"What do you mean?"

"A few people saw you jump bad on her at the Phi party a while back."

"What are you talking about?" asked Kendall innocently, but realizing exactly what Linda was referring to.

"Soror, I didn't see it, but rumor on the yard is that you snatched Tina off the dance floor when TJ got a little out of hand."

"What's wrong with that? I was trying to protect her from his drunk ass."

"Are you sure?"

"Yeah, why?"

Linda hesitated, so Kendall asked again, "Why?"

"Well … some people are saying that it looked like a lover's quarrel between you and Tina. And they're also saying you damn near pimp-slapped her."

"I …"

"And they're also saying that the two of you stay up in your apartment all the time because you're more that just roommates." Linda swallowed.

"What?"

"They're saying that you and Tina are kickin' it on the real," Linda said. "Look, I'm just gonna ask you, are you and Tina sleeping together?"

"Linda, I can't believe you just asked me that!"

"Soror, if I can't ask you, nobody can. Now tell me something so I can set these fools on the yard straight," Linda pleaded.

"I am not sleeping with Tina," Kendall lied.

"You sure?"

"Look dammit, I said I'm not sleeping with her. Now if you'll excuse me, I have some studying to do," Kendall said as she got up from the table.

"I know. We're s'pose to be studying together."

"Yeah, well, all of a sudden I don't feel so well. I need to be alone."

"You sure? I didn't mean to upset you."

"Naw, it's straight. I'll be fine. I'll call you later."

As Linda was leaving, I came home.

"Hey, Linda. What's up?" I smiled.

"Uh. I think I just upset Kendall a little bit."

"What happened?"

"She'll tell you. I'll see you later," Linda said as she walked away.

I silently entered the apartment unsure but unafraid of Kendall's mood.

"Kendall?"

"In here," she answered. I walked into the dining room to see Kendall holding her head in her hands.

"What's up, girl?" I asked.

"They know."

"They know what?"

"The yard. It's out on the yard."

"What's out on the yard?"

"Rumors about you and me."

"Oh," I said as I sank down into a chair. "How?"

"They saw me when I confronted you on the dance floor the other week. They saw the chemistry between you and me and I guess the rumors just took off from there."

"Who saw it?"

"Nobody. Everybody. I don't know."

"Damn."

"I told Linda it's not true."

I sat in silence with my head resting on the back of the chair. "What do you want to do?"

"Nothing. Deny it. Get out more. Separately."

"Why, Kendall?"

"Why what?" she asked.

"Why deny it?"

"Because … we're not ready."

"We're not ready or you're not ready?"

"We're not ready."

"Maybe I am," I replied.

"When did you get so comfortable with it?"

"Just now."

"Why?"

I paused for a moment before I responded. " I want the world to know that I love you. I'm tired of hiding it. What do we have to lose?"

"What do we have to lose? We'll be ridiculed and laughed at. Folks will call us queer, dykes, and lesbians. You're ready for that?"

"If loving you means I am a lesbian, then yes, I'm ready to deal with it."

"Well, I'm not, Tina. I'm not going public."

"Fine."

"Fine."

I walked out of the room and left Kendall to her thoughts. I had my own to deal with. What was really so bad with making it known that Kendall and I were a couple? Yes, we'd be teased and laughed at. People would stare and point. Fellas would probably try to step to us even harder or invite themselves to a threesome. But so what, they try to do that anyway! The hardest part would be dealing with our respective sorors, but we could do it. I'm sure of it. If people wanted to label me as gay then so be it. Maybe I am.

Kendall slept in her own room that night. She was mad at the world and I wasn't trying to deal with her attitude. But as I rubbed the empty spot in my bed where she ordinarily lay, I realized that I missed her. For a brief moment I pictured my future without her and I didn't like the way it made me feel.

The Cop-out
TINA

When I awoke the next morning Kendall was already gone. This was highly unusual considering the fact that she rarely sees early morning sunlight.

I was in the kitchen pouring myself a glass of juice before I headed to work when in walked Kendall. With TJ. They were giggling and didn't notice me at first. Perhaps it was my wide-mouth stare, furrowed eyebrows, and increasing vibes of anger that finally got their attention.

"Tina! I didn't realize you were still home," said Kendall.

"Apparently," I replied stonily.

"Hey, Tina. You're looking fine as usual," said TJ.

"Thanks," I said through clenched teeth.

"Umm … we just got in from Mika and Taj's party," said Kendall.

"That's nice. Have a nice time?" I asked not really caring to hear the answer.

"It was decent," said TJ.

Finally, I just asked the question, "What are you doing here, TJ?"

"Oh. Kendall said she'd hook me up with some breakfast this morning," he said as he rubbed her arm.

"Is that right?" I asked as I gave Kendall an icy glare. "And what will you be preparing, Kendall?"

"I'm not sure," she said as she looked at the floor. "What's in the fridge?"

"Nothing."

"Oh," Kendall said as she continued to stare at the floor, then the wall, but never once meeting my eyes.

"We can skip the breakfast, Kendall, but can I still get that massage you promised me?"

"Get the fuck out of my house, TJ," I said.

"'Xcuse me?" he said.

"Get out."

TJ looked from me to Kendall and back to me. "Yo, I guess what they're saying on the yard is true. Y'all doing it like that? D-aaammmnnnn!" TJ started laughing.

"TJ, you better leave," said Kendall.

"I'm out. Tina, don't be mad. Maybe we can talk about doing a three." He was still laughing as he walked out the door.

The tension in the room was thick.

"I can explain," Kendall started.

"No. You can't explain shit to me. One minute you love me. The next minute you're jealous. And the next minute you're bringing dudes up in our home! There's not a damn thing to explain! I wish to hell that you never would have slipped and fell. You have turned my world upside down, inside out, and side-to-side. And for what?"

"Tina," Kendall interrupted.

"You know what, Kendall? When I told you I was in love with you, I didn't lie. I was willing to risk everything for you. Thank you for helping me to realize what a huge mistake that would have been." And then I left. I went straight to work and rather than study afterwards, I looked for a new place to live. By five o'clock that afternoon I had put a deposit down on a small one-bedroom apartment way off campus. It would be ready by the start of the next semester which was less than two weeks away.

When I got home Kendall was there. She apparently skipped her class and had prepared dinner. It smelled like steak, but I didn't stop in the kitchen to investigate. Instead I walked straight to my room.

"Tina, we need to talk," Kendall said as she followed me.

"Really? What about?"

"This morning. Last night. Us."

"There's nothing to talk about."

"Please, Tina. Just listen."

"No. This time, I'm going to listen to my head instead of my heart. By the way, I think you should know I'll be moving out in about two weeks. I'm not going to renew the lease for this apartment."

"Tina, don't move. Don't break this lease and fuck up your finances. You're not thinking straight. You're mad at me and you're reacting without thinking."

"I already signed the contract. It's about time for you to head back to State anyway."

"Dammit, Tina, I moved here to be with you! I know I messed up. I told you from jump that I didn't know how to deal with this. I told you I was afraid. I'm not as strong as you. I'm afraid of what people will say." Kendall was crying.

"You know what, Kendall? I'm afraid, too. To my knowledge, there's no manual that details how to openly live without criticism and ridicule with your same-sex lover! But I'm dealing with it, Kendall! At least I was willing to try. Willing to fight for you. For us. You gave up without even trying!"

Kendall was crying hard by this point so I continued. "I'm not gay, Kendall. At least, that's what I keep telling myself. Right now, I consider myself open to exploration and love. What we're doing, what I've been doing, is exploring. And you know what?" I didn't wait for her to answer. "I have thoroughly enjoyed my discovery! If we had explored together for the rest of our lives, it would be okay with me! I'd even call myself a lesbian. I'd commit to you and only you. I'd love you completely with all of my mind, body, and soul. And I wouldn't give a damn what anybody outside of these walls had to say. The funny part, Kendall, is that I've already confessed my love to you! So, in my opinion, I'm probably halfway there to lesbian-hood!

"I'm willing to confront my fears, but you aren't. Why, baby girl? Isn't love supposed to conquer all? I don't know … Maybe you don't love me as much as you think you do 'cause if you did, we wouldn't be standing here right now having this conversation. The worst part is that on top of all the uncertainty and madness … is a friendship dissolved." I walked closer and closer to Kendall. When I was right in front of her, less than an inch from her face, I kissed her. I tilted my head to the right, leaned forward, and very tenderly sucked on her lips. The kiss was much like the kiss that Kendall placed on my lips when we began our relationship. How ironic, then, that the kiss I placed on her lips was a kiss goodbye.

On My Own
TINA

After the kiss goodbye, I packed as much of my stuff as I could and temporarily moved in with my sands Tranay until my new apartment was ready. I also came clean with my sorority sisters: yes, I slept with Kendall. To my surprise, they supported me. They didn't understand why I'd want to have sex with a female, but they still supported me.

Thanks to TJ, the entire yard was talking about Kendall and me. Some folks laughed. Some joked. Some pointed. I think some even silently understood. But no one ever said anything directly to me. Maybe they knew that I just didn't give a fuck.

Two weeks later, when summer school was over and the new semester was officially under way and the majority of the students were back from their break, most of the talk about Kendall and me had died down. I successfully moved into my apartment and life was pretty much back to normal.

I didn't date at all during that semester. I basically went to class, went to work, studied, and worked out.

Believe it or not, these four things kept me fairly busy.

I heard that Kendall had transferred back to State. Many times I wanted to reach out to her, call her or send her a text message, but I couldn't bring myself to do it. Stubborn.

I didn't party as much as I used to, but I did manage to go out once right before finals. I was lining around the dance floor like sorority girls do. I had on a bad black dress with a diamond cut out of the middle front. It showed my tight abs and even a glimpse of my belly ring. The dress was short so it revealed my long legs and a lot of well-muscled thigh. I looked good.

I felt a familiar stare. As I looked around to try and find the source of the stare, I eventually found myself looking directly into the eyes of Kendall. She was leaning against the wall talking to a guy. I can't recall his name. As I got closer to where she was standing, her gaze never left mine and I detected a longing in her stare. But there was something else present. If I didn't know any better, I'd think Kendall was trying to convey to me that she missed me. And as I passed her by, because I was still in my sorority line, I tried to send her a sign that I missed her, too.

When the party was over I went home. Alone. As I walked up the stairs to my apartment, I was shocked to find Kendall sitting on the ground outside my door.

"Kendall!"

"Tina, can we talk?"

"Yeah," I said as I unlocked the door. "Come in."

Kendall followed me into my apartment.

"It's bigger than I thought it would be. But it's tidy, just as I suspected," she smiled.

"How'd you know where I lived?"

"Come on, Tina. This campus isn't that big! Plus I drove by here several times before I headed back to State hoping I might run into you."

"What are you doing here?"

"I miss you, Tina."

I nodded with understanding. "I miss you, too. But why are you here?" I asked again.

"I'm ready," she said.

"Ready for what?"

"Ready to openly love you." I sat down as she continued. "I've been miserable without you. It wasn't because of the snickers and the pointing. Surprisingly, that wasn't too bad. The horrible part was living without you.

"Tina, we had a friendship before we had a relationship. Our friendship followed by the few short months we spent together as lovers was the best time of my life. You made me feel special. You made me feel loved. You did love me. And I truly regret not being able to love you back – the way you deserved," Kendall said as she sat down on the couch beside me.

"Dammit, Kendall. I'm trying to get over you."

"Have you been with anyone else since me?"

"No."

"Me neither. Would you like to know why?"

"Why?"

"Because there's no one else I'd rather be with." She looked into my eyes. A tear rolled down my face as I listened to her speak. "Don't cry." She wiped away my tear.

"We've already been through this, Kendall. It's too late."

"Are you sure? Does it have to be?"

"I already kissed you goodbye. I can't open my heart back up only to get hurt again," I said. Love has a price tag. What price was I willing to pay to let it walk away?

"Can I ask you something?"

"Yes."

"Do you love me?"

"Yes."

"I love you too, Tina. I'll always love you. And I'm sorry that I didn't love you right when I had the chance." There was an uncomfortable silence. Kendall reached over and pulled me into a hug. Her hand softly touched the weak spot on the back of my neck. Then she kissed me on my cheek.

"Take care, Tina."

"I will," I said. And just like that, a chapter of my life was closed.

With Regrets
KENDALL

My life is miserable without Tina. What was I thinking when I brought TJ home that morning? I had no intention of making him breakfast or giving him a massage. And while I knew his mind was thinking about my booty, I definitely wasn't going to give it up to him! I just wanted the yard to see me in public with a guy. I just wanted them to focus on something other than my private life at home with Tina. How could I have been so stupid?

While I think Tina is very attractive, it was not my intent to fall for or on her. There is no scientific explanation for why I kissed her. Up until my first kiss with Tina, I never once felt attracted to other females. I wasn't raised by homosexual parents. I was never molested as a child. These are the two excuses I hear when naysayers try to explain homosexuality. Hell, I had been strictly dickly up until the moment I fell on top of her.

Something happened within me when my body met hers. It was electrical. It was sobering. And it was very natural. Laying on top of her and staring into her crazy cat-like eyes and her beautiful, soft, full lips, made me think I was going to lose my mind. Through all our years of friendship, I had seen Tina in various states of undress and I had laid beside her countless times. But something was different this time.

I think she tried to get up, but I shifted my body so that I could stare for a moment longer 'cause I felt like I'd never be that close to perfection again. And her eyes. They mesmerized me. Then she parted her lips. Maybe she simply inhaled. Whatever it was, whatever she intended, I took it for an invitation. So I gently bent down and softly sucked her bottom lip. I couldn't help myself. After I did it, I could not believe that I had the audacity to kiss a female without even asking for permission! Even if it was just a little kiss. I quickly pushed myself off of her and apologized.

Tina was so quiet. How unusual for my friend who is known to unleash a wicked tongue when she feels that justice has not been done. She was probably trying to decide which cuss words would be most effective for this situation. She shook her head and sat up. I thought she was going to swing on me so I jumped up because I knew I was way out of line. But she didn't swing on me. Instead she took my hand and pulled it downward. She was quietly suggesting that I sit down on the floor next to her.

I couldn't tell what she was thinking and it was driving me crazy. I stole a glance at her and her normally green eyes looked hazel and cloudy. She didn't look angry, but one can never be certain when dealing with a person who has eyes that appear to change color with the slightest change in temperature. Again,

I told her I was sorry. She still didn't say anything. Ten seconds seemed like an eternity. I felt tears forming in my eyes. She finally stood up and reached down with her hand to help me stand. We almost stood eye-to-eye, but Tina was slightly taller than I. I felt a tear fall. Tina gently brushed it away with one hand and with the other she brushed my cheek.

I watched as she closed her eyes, parted her lips to inhale, and allowed her lips to descend upon mine. As I sighed, my lips parted and our tongues introduced themselves to one another. I didn't want to stop, but she said, "Do you want to do this?"

I said, "I've never done anything like this before, Tina."

"Me, neither."

She looked deep into my eyes and down at my lips. She grabbed my hand and led me to her room. We sat down on the bed and from there, each step was one of learning. We undressed each other and openly admired all that was before us. Tina's skin, a beautiful brown hue, reminiscent of a warm cup of hot chocolate, beckoned for me to touch it. Taste it. Explore it.

I had no idea what I was doing. I just went with the flow. I did whatever seemed natural. I used my instincts and followed the yearnings of her body. When I was done pleasing her, she pleased me. We spoke no words. We just knew. I had never been so fulfilled as I was that night and the following morning with Tina.

For the first time in a long time, I witnessed the sun rise.

"Tina?"

"Hmm?"

"I've never done anything like that before."

"Me, neither, but I've always wanted to. Did you enjoy it?"

"Do you even have to ask?"

"What now?" Tina asked me.

I didn't have an answer for her because I didn't know what would happen next. Then she brought up Tonio and Marcus, our boyfriends, and my mind just went blank.

Then she asked me, "Kendall, had you thought about me before tonight?"

I don't think that I fully comprehended the depth of her question. But at that point, it didn't matter so I said, "Yes."

She seemed pleased with my answer. We then vowed to not let this night of experimentation ruin our friendship. We snuggled some more and fell asleep.

I heard the banging on the door, but I require an absolute minimum of eight hours of sleep each night. Therefore, I didn't make any effort to get up and answer the unrelenting - and unnecessary - pounding. Tina, on the other hand, is fully functional with little or no sleep. I don't know how she does it. The girl is definitely high-energy. Sure enough, I felt her slide out of my arms and put on her slippers and robe. When she got to the door and opened it, I heard Tonio's deep baritone voice. I immediately sat up. What if he came into the room? Were those my yellow panties on Tina's desk? I didn't want to make any noise so I just sat there and quietly wrapped the sheet around me.

I heard their entire conversation. Tina lied to her man about three times in an effort to protect me. Us.

In between the lies Tina came into her room to get Tonio's economics book, which was indeed under my panties. She came to me and touched my hair. Then she went back out to him.

I laid down and rubbed my temples. What were we thinking last night? She eventually came back and lay beside me.

Again I apologized to her. She didn't want an apology. She said our actions the night before were a mutual decision. The question that loomed over us was whether one night, one act, meant that we were gay. Neither of us had an answer to that question and neither one of us knew what to do next.

I Love You

KENDALL

As hard as we tried, returning to life as we had known it before that magical night was close to impossible. What Tina and I shared that night was spontaneous, yet it almost seemed destined to happen. So trying to pretend like it was a one-time deal was ridiculous.

We made a quick decision that I should transfer to U for summer school. It made sense. She was there, my boyfriend was there, I was down there every weekend anyway, and they had a good business school. Once there, though, I was stressed. It seemed like I noticed Tina more now that we had shared an evening of intimacy together. No matter where I went on the yard, there she was. No matter what class I was in or what dream I was having, she was on my mind. No matter how hard I tried not to gaze upon her chest or make physical contact with her when passing, I did.

I looked forward to having dinner with her and studying together on the couch. I liked it when she laid her head in my lap and I played in her long, thick black hair as we watched tv.

Each evening as she'd exit the bathroom after a long hot shower following her nightly exercise romp at the gym, it was all I could do to contain myself from following her towel-wrapped body to her bedroom. The thoughts that filled my head were absolutely non-Christian and some would definitely call them sinful. My grandparents would turn over in their graves if they could see and hear the things that I was fantasizing about. Even with all the touching and cuddling, Tina and I didn't kiss or have sex again. It was a mutual decision that neither one of us ever voiced. It was driving me crazy.

So there I was, wanting to get physically close to Tina again while denying my boyfriend of two years, Marcus, at the same time. Truth be told, he was pissing me off with all of his whining. I was supposed to be studying, but instead of taking notes, I was drawing hearts with Tina's name in them. How juvenile is that?

I felt her staring at me long before I turned to acknowledge her presence. When I did finally turn towards her, she looked troubled.

"What's wrong, Tina?"

"Nothing." I could tell she was lying.

"You sure?"

"No," she said as she walked into my room and sat on my bed. I went and sat beside her. Tina opened up to me that evening and I learned that I wasn't the only one distressed about our situation. She was feeling me just as much as I was feeling her. The primary difference between how we were feeling was that Tina was more willing to go public and openly express how she felt about me. I wasn't. I also learned that Tina had been attracted to women before, but she never acted on it. Lastly, I admitted to myself and to Tina that I was in love with her. I think I fell for her from the very first kiss. It sounded odd to voice to a woman that I was in love with her, but my words were true. As she wrapped her thick, long, jean-covered legs around my waist, I wanted her. I needed to show her how very true my words were.

Then she said, "Prove it." And I did.

For You

KENDALL

After I made love to Tina, in my room this time, we decided that we should end our relationships with our existing boyfriends. I repeatedly asked Tina if she was sure she wanted to end her three-year relationship with a future professional football player. Tina said she was sure so I stopped questioning her.

It wasn't that difficult for me to end my two-year relationship with Marcus. I had put up with more shit during the past two years than I wanted to admit. He had cheated on me numerous times and he was on his way to becoming an alcoholic.

Marcus was a fine-ass red-boned playa who sported a fade and a goatee. Jeans and gym shoes were his standard attire. It always bothered me that his chest and ass were hairy. And the sex wasn't even that good. I didn't love Marcus. I think I stayed with him out of pure convenience. I knew I could do better.

I went to his apartment the afternoon after I declared my love to Tina. As usual, Marcus was watching tv, a basketball game, and drinking a six-pack of beer. I sat down on his raggedy gold couch. Yes, I said gold. "Marcus, I think I need some space."

"Some space? What you mean?" He burped.

"I mean, I need to be solo for a while."

"Alright then, shawty."

Just like that, it was over. I wanted to kick myself for wasting so much time with this loser. I got up to leave and Marcus said, "Leave your key." I placed his key on the table and walked out. No tears. No kiss goodbye. Just freedom.

Tina and I decided to go home for the weekend to check in on our families. I had planned on spending the time lounging with my much older parents. I spend as much time as I can with my parents because I know they're on the down side of life. My dad especially. His memory is getting worse and worse. And his arthritis is not something to take lightly, either.

When Tina called shortly after we arrived home, I was somewhat alarmed. She didn't explain what was wrong, she just said she needed to go back to school early. I was really in a dilemma because I had planned on spending the time at home doing some things around the house for my folks. I also wanted to sit down and talk to my mom about my dad's recent doctor appointment. She had mentioned to me, during a telephone call after his appointment, that he may be experiencing the early onset of Alzheimer's disease. I was really looking forward to spending some quality time with my parents and making sure that all was well with them.

Yet, it seemed like Tina, my friend before anything else, needed a friend. So without a moment's notice, I told her I'd ride back with her. She had no idea about the plans that I would have to cancel or the sadness this would bring to both me and my parents. Instead, she said, "Okay. I'll pick you up in a few."

Jealousy Has Green Eyes
KENDALL

Back at school, Tina went about the arduous task of finding a part-time job. I already had a position with a local CPA firm. I spent most of my free time coming up with different sexual things for Tina and me to try. I mean, let's face it, neither one of us had the body tools that were historically believed to be the only devices that could satisfy a woman. However, let it be stated and time-stamped here, that utilization of a penis is not the only way in which to keep a woman sexually satisfied. Tina and I found many ways to please each other and none of them involved a dick.

As relationships go, we had our ups and downs. We basically got into the same arguments as lovers that we did when we were best friends. Tina is a neat freak. She believes that everything has a place, dishes should be washed after each meal, beds should be made each day, and bathrooms should be cleaned after each use. Interesting.

I, on the other hand, come from the mindset that change is good, but less is more. Dishes should be washed when you run out of them or when somebody else does them. Beds are just going to get messed up again so why waste your time making them neat and crisp? And bathrooms should be cleaned weekly, not daily. I can't tell you how many times we clashed over these things, yet we always managed to compromise. For example, as long as I scrape the uneaten food off the dish, place it in the sink and not on the counter, Tina will wash it. I clean the bathroom every Saturday. If she wants to clean it more frequently, that's on her.

Tina's shortcomings are in the financial arena. She never balances her checkbook and the bill collectors have our phone number on a weekly rotation because they're always calling to remind her that something is past due. To relieve her of her financial inattentiveness, I took over her checkbook. I balance it, write her checks out for her, and mail them.

The one thing that Tina does pay attention to is her body. Tina has a body that cannot be reckoned with; it's sculpted and toned, shaved and polished. She puts a lot of effort into making sure her body is right and her clothing is tight (literally and figuratively). Her clothing selection is usually quite tasteful, but that doesn't stop the haters from hatin'. There are several females on the yard who are jealous as hell of Tina's total package. And most of the male population on campus wants to bed her down.

Almost immediately into summer session the Phi's had a party that was all the way live. Brothas were drunk. People were sweating. The music was bumping. The party was just straight up bananas.

I was lining around the party as black Greeks are known to do. Tina was on the dance floor with a Phi named TJ. As usual, TJ was drunk and high and acting like an ass.

This particular night Tina had on a really nice white halter top that tied around her neck and didn't quite cover her stomach. Her belly button is pierced and you could see the diamond glittering with the right light. And she had on some tight black shorts. The outfit was simple, but it was driving the brothas in the room crazy.

TJ was holding Tina's waist and grinding all into her pelvic area. She would politely back away or remove his hands, but I have to give it to him as he was persistent – every time she backed away, he moved forward. So I was doing my thing with my sorors when I notice TJ cup both cheeks of Tina's ass, pull her into him and gyrate in a very, very provocative manner. I can't explain what went off inside of my head, but I can explain what I did. I politely stepped out of my line, twitched my skinny self with my tight black dress over to where they were dancing, grabbed Tina by the wrist, and pulled her off to the side of the party.

"What the hell, Tina? Why don't you just fuck him on the dance floor?" I shouted.

"Kendall," Tina said as quietly as she could through clenched teeth, "what the hell is wrong with you?" She glanced around to see if anybody was watching us.

"What's wrong? What's wrong? I don't appreciate watching TJ suggest that y'all should be more than dance partners!" I yelled.

"Kendall," Tina smiled, but anyone who was paying attention could tell that she was angry, "I do not want to have this conversation with you right now."

Then, just like that, I snapped back into the "be normal while you're out in public mode." Later, when we left the party, Tina was hot. She made many valid points on the ride home, but I was trippin' over myself as I realized that I was so into this girl that I could get jealous at the drop of a dime. I guess it didn't hurt that I also had heard on the yard that TJ was going to try and give Tina some play now that she and Tonio were no longer an item. When I tried to make this notion a part of my defense, it sounded weak. Tina, never being one to hold her tongue, set me straight real quick.

I finally just admitted to her that I was jealous. I should have stopped there. Why was it that I couldn't think straight when I was around this girl? Was I pussy-whipped? All signs would point to yes. I'll never know why I mentioned that she should be more selective in her choice of clothing during this conversation, but I did. Talk about stupid! I really set her off when I mentioned her clothes. She was so pissed that she marched out of my room and into hers and she slammed the door behind her. We had never had any door-slamming in our house before.

I put my robe on and followed her to her room. I knocked before I went in. When I opened the door and saw Tina standing there with fire in her green eyes, she looked sexy as hell. That's the only way I can explain it. Suddenly the fight didn't matter. All I wanted to do was kiss my girl's sexy-ass lips.

I approached her slowly and was willing to say whatever she needed me to say. I just needed to have her in my arms. I walked behind her and half licked, half kissed the back of her neck. All of our experimenting had taught me that her neck, the back of her neck in particular, was one of her most sensitive spots. Tina asked me to stop, but I saw her weakening so I kissed the spot right between her breasts. She said something. I agreed and untied her top, but I didn't let it fall because I needed to make it clear that yes, I was wrong tonight. Once Tina was satisfied with my apology and forgave me for my thoughtless actions, only then did she allow me to devour her femininity.

Scared To Just Be

KENDALL

If I could take back that night where I was clearly at fault and overreacted to TJ's drunken, mindless roamings ... If I could take back my all-nighter at Mika and Taj's party without letting Tina know where I was ... If I could take back the fact that I brought TJ inside of Tina's and my coveted closed doors ... I would.

Life is cruel, though, and second chances don't come often. And Tina's not the type to tolerate a bunch of mess. Mess, however, is exactly what I gave her, from the untidy apartment to the jealousy to the inability to openly acknowledge her.

I knew what I was doing when I brought TJ home. I was ending our relationship. But that doesn't make it right. I miss Tina so much. I didn't lie to her when I first told her I loved her. I did, however, lie to her and myself when I wouldn't admit that I was gay. Because contrary to my thoughtless actions, I wanted to be with her for the rest of my life. But at that moment, I wasn't strong enough to admit it. My mouth wouldn't form the words.

SHE *Slipped* AND FELL

I avoided Tina on the yard after she broke up with me. There was no point in seeking her out 'cause I knew she didn't want to have anything else to do with me. I packed up my stuff and headed back to State dejected and alone. It was a long semester.

I traveled back to U at the end of the fall semester at the request of my sorors for a party. I prayed the entire ride down that Tina wouldn't be there. Luck, however, was not on my side because Tina was there and she looked amazing. She had on a simple black dress with a diamond cut out of the front. Its simplicity made it sexy. She wore it well. I tried not to stare, but I couldn't help myself. This girl would have loved me openly if I would have allowed her to. I was such an idiot. I stared too long. Tina's green eyes met mine. I think she was trying to tell me something. Could she tell that I was still in love with her?

I knew where she lived so I left the party early and waited outside her door. The evening air had a chill in it, but I sat on the ground and waited anyway. The thought never occurred to me to sit in my car where I could turn the heat on. Nor did it ever occur to me that she might bring someone home with her. I was relieved when she finally arrived. Alone.

She was surprised to see me, but she let me come in. Her place was cute and tidy. I told her as much. I didn't go to the apartment expecting her to take me back. I knew that she wouldn't. I went to her apartment to apologize for all the wrong I had done and to let her know that she would always be my one true love.

ATL

TINA

Life in Atlanta, Georgia, was everything that I thought it would be. It was fast-paced. There was lots of traffic and lots of people. The weather was nice compared to what I was used to in the Midwest.

I was surprised to learn that the city of Atlanta is actually quite small, but the suburbs around it are what make it seem like such a metropolis. Decatur, College Park, Marietta, Powder Springs, Roswell – they're all separate and distinct cities, yet they're all considered extensions of Atlanta.

Another thing I learned about Atlanta that didn't quite make sense was the number of streets called "Peachtree." How could one city have so many streets with the same name and they didn't even connect? It was confusing as hell.

Oh, and if you asked somebody how far point A is from point B, the standard answer is twenty minutes. I don't care if you are on the south side of I-285 and headed to the north side, the city folks down there swear it only takes twenty minutes to get anywhere.

SHE *Slipped* AND FELL

Damn liars! Their lack of time awareness almost made me late for an interview.

I found a small apartment in downtown Decatur. I also found a part-time job to pay the rent and buy groceries. Once school started my hours were consumed with studying and work. I no longer got to work out every day like I used to because I was typically far too tired. But I did manage to buy a couple of aerobic tapes and a bike. My apartment was only three miles from campus so when the weather was nice, I could ride my bike to class. I also maintained a healthy diet so I didn't feel too guilty about the lack of daily exercise.

I met a few people who were in the same program as I at Unity University. Lazarus Daniels is a light-complected, medium-build brother with a big booty who's studying pediatric medicine like myself. He's from Oklahoma and is country as hell, but he's sweet. His smile is to die for. He reminds me of Tonio.

Nicole Perez is a half black, half Hispanic sister from San Antonio, Texas. She's more urban than Lazarus, but not much. Nicole wants to be a pediatric heart doctor. Very specialized. She has a ten-year-old sister who has suffered three heart attacks since birth. None of the doctors can figure out what's wrong with her. Nicole made a vow that she'd figure it out. I've never seen such determination. I believe she'll do it.

The last person to round out our group is Miguel Estrada. He, too, is Hispanic but his parents are actual immigrants. He's lived in Miami since the age of eight. Miguel is my neighbor and he's majoring in immigration law. He wants to help immigrants successfully cross over onto American soil.

These three – Lazarus, Nicole, and Miguel - were my first friends in Atlanta. Together we study, eat and sometimes we even manage to catch a movie. It was just a matter of time before we coupled up. Nicole and Miguel started dating first – they were really feelin' each other. I think Laz and I hooked up out of pure convenience.

If you take intimacy out of the equation, Lazarus and I have the perfect relationship. He has a sense of humor, he's smart, and he's considerate. Throw intimacy in the mix, though, and the relationship dims considerably. The first kiss Lazarus and I shared was not impressive. It was way too wet and far too sloppy. I wasn't sure if that was the way Oklahoma folks did it or if I simply felt a need to compare his every move to Kendall. Plus, I've learned that he's only had three girlfriends his entire life. He had his first girlfriend when he was in first grade. No surprise there. He lost his virginity to his second girlfriend whom he dated while getting his undergrad. And now there's me. I am his second sexual experience which ultimately explains his lack of skills in the bedroom.

Lazarus only handles the task at hand. In, out, no foreplay. It's nerve-racking and far from satisfying. I will admit that I'm somewhat comforted knowing that he can get better with practice and patience, but I'm not certain that I want to be the one to help improve his craftsmanship in the bedroom. So I avoid intimacy with him as often as possible.

Coursework at Unity is no joke. Biochemistry, genetics, inorganic chemistry, gross anatomy … I am certain that my first gray hair sprouted as a result of these classes! Even so, I somehow manage to remain on top of it all. A lot of it is my determination not to fail. And it doesn't hurt to have a good support network via Lazarus, Nicole, and Miguel. By helping each other study and stay focused, we all made it through our first full year of post-undergrad successfully.

Back Home

KENDALL

I moved back home after graduation. Moving back home was a financial help to me and a physical help to my parents. I didn't have any problems settling in. My parents never questioned my whereabouts and they respected my privacy. All in all, life was good.

The first thing I did after I got my things situated at the house was find a job. I had a recommendation from the accountant I worked for during the summer I was at U. Thanks to his glowing words, I was immediately hired on as an accounting assistant at a moderate-sized firm. If I passed my CPA exam, they would promote me to a junior accountant. I planned on studying for the test and taking it six months down the road. The sooner I got promoted to junior accountant, the more money in my paycheck and hence the sooner I could pay off my student loans.

As much as I hated to get up early, every day of the workweek I was at the office by eight o'clock. My workday concluded at five. I didn't really care for my boss. He was a smug, toothpick-skinny, non-attractive male who believed he was God's gift to women. What a joke! But whatever, I wasn't trying to date the man. As a matter o fact, dating was the last thing on my mind. All I wanted was a paycheck. Cha-ching! When my workday was over, I'd go home where I would undoubtedly walk into a house that smelled like Sunday dinner.

"Mama, you have got to stop cooking these elaborate meals! As a matter of fact, you don't have to cook for me at all. I can't eat like this every day. I'll get as big as this house!"

"Honey, I don't mind. Cooking makes me happy."

"Your cooking is going to make me fat! Seriously, Mama, don't cook like this just because I'm back home. I can eat salad. And then, some days, I'm not even hungry."

"You sound like your daddy. I guess y'all don't like my cooking anymore," Mama said with her head bowed.

"That's not it. You know you can throw down in the kitchen! I don't know what Daddy's reasons are, but mine is simple: I just can't eat a big Sunday dinner every day of the week."

Mama giggled then she seemed to have a lightbulb go off in her head as she said, "Or are you trying to stay thin and catch you a man? I need some grandbabies soon while I'm still young enough to enjoy them."

"Mama, you are way off base. No boyfriends, husbands, or babies for me right now. I want to pay off my student loans, save some money, and travel a bit before I even think about settling down."

"Well, you can't blame your poor mama for trying."

As time went by I settled into a routine. Work from eight to five. Dinner with the folks. I cleaned up the kitchen for them every night, but I credit my actions to the assistance of the dishwasher. After I cleaned up the kitchen we'd sit down and watch tv. Sometimes I'd read a book while they watched tv. Some evenings we'd go shopping. Whatever the event, I always shared my weekday evenings with my folks. I loved and appreciated them and I wanted them to know it.

On Saturdays I slept in. I typically didn't get out of bed till noon. When I did, Mama and Daddy were long gone out doing Saturday-type stuff. I'd clean the house and wash my clothes. I pretty much did nothing. My parents must have been worried about me because one Saturday, as I chatted with a stranger on my laptop, my dad said something to me.

"Kendall, how come you never go anywhere? Out with your friends?" he asked.

"Daddy, I went out enough in college to last me a lifetime."

"But, honey, you don't get any phone calls, you don't make any calls. Where are all your friends?"

"We've all gone our separate ways."

"What's Tina up to lately? Y'all used to clown around here all the time."

"Daddy, remember I told you, she's down south. In Atlanta."

"What about them fraternity girls?"

"Sorority girls? I don't know. I haven't kept in touch with anyone. I'm not ready to get active with the alumnae chapter yet. I'm just chillin' right now."

"Hmmpf. I don't think it's natural for a young woman as beautiful as you are to be home all the time just chillin'. Don't you get tired of looking at me and yo mama?"

I stood up from the chair I was sitting in and walked towards my dad. I reached down and gently pinched his weary, sagging cheeks. "How could I ever get tired of looking at this face?" I asked.

"Hell, I get tired of looking at this wrinkled, old face. Yo mama gets tired of looking at it 'cause she tells me every chance she gets. So it would stand to reason that you get tired of it, too."

"Nope. I'm not."

"Well, Kendall, what about a man? Are you seeing somebody? Maybe at work?"

"Nope."

"Why not?"

"Not interested."

"Girl, when me and yo mama was your age, we was already married."

"Uh-huh. That's why mama's tired of looking at your face, old man!" I laughed. Daddy shook his head and walked away.

I sat back down, typed a response to the instant message on my laptop, and then looked out the family room window. My parents were really trippin' about my social life or lack thereof. Why? I really was content. I liked being around my folks. I've always been a loner so the fact that I didn't hang out with a bunch of friends all the time did not bother me in the slightest.

And a relationship? After the break-up with Tina, a relationship wasn't foreseeable at any point in the near future. I wasn't ready for the emotional baggage that comes along with a relationship. Besides, I think that deep down inside, if I explored my feelings, I'd find that Tina was still very much a part of my heart.

Mia

TINA

One year down, three to go. Then I'd be done with med school. But after med school I still have to complete my residency. What the hell was I thinking when I decided that I wanted to become a doctor?

I have no social life! I have good grades, but no social life. It's driving me crazy. I yearn to slip into a tight little number with high heels and make my mark on this city called Atlanta. Every time I ask Laz if he wants to go out, he says no, the nightlife isn't for him. Nicole always declines my invitation, too, as she is truly focused on her books. I get the feeling Miguel would go if I asked him, but how would that look? So, every time I get the urge to get my groove on and shake my tailfeather, I go for a run or to the gym instead. At least I'm maintaining my body.

It was a Saturday afternoon and I was at a small coffee shop right off campus sipping on a latte and studying microbiology when I peeped a sister wearing my sorority colors and letters out of the corner of my eye. Why hadn't I thought of that before? My sorors.

They're probably all over Atlanta. Maybe they could help me regain my social life.

I watched her over the rim of my cup as I took another sip. She made her purchase at the register and found a corner table to rest herself. I waited until she looked comfortable, closed my book, put it in my bag, drained the last of my latte, stood, put my bag over my shoulder, and walked towards my soror.

"Excuse me, I couldn't help but notice your Greeks and as your soror, I wanted to introduce myself. My name is Tina Jones, Mu Chapter," I said as I extended my hand for the sacred sorority handshake.

The soror stood and gently shook my hand and then pulled me in for a hug which is customary for sorors to do whether you know them or not. "Hey," she said. "My name is Mia. I'm a graduate student at Unity and a member of the Atlanta Alumnae Chapter. It's nice to meet you. Have a seat?"

"I would like to, but I really can't stay long. I saw your Greeks and just wanted to acknowledge you. I've been in Atlanta for a year now; my head has been so deep in my books that I don't get to go out much. I never see sorors anywhere – be it on the yard at Unity, at the grocery ... nowhere."

"Well, girl, we're here and we're in full effect. It sounds like you're not active with the alumnae chapter."

"I don't have time!"

"I hear you. What's your major?"

"Med school: pediatrics."

"No wonder you don't have time! Let me get your number and e-mail. I can keep you posted on happenings and events. If you ever get a break, we meet the first Saturday of every month. The location typically varies, but I'll give you my contact info. That way, should you decide you want to attend, just give me a call or shoot me an e-mail."

"That'll be great. Thanks, Mia!" I said as I bent to write down my number on a piece of paper that Mia handed me. She wrote her info down, then we exchanged information.

I folded the paper and was about to slip it in my bag when Mia said, "Just so you know, next Saturday afternoon we're hosting a 'For The Kids Party' for children with sickle cell anemia. Several community leaders are going to be there. You should come. Afterwards, the sorors will probably go clubbin'."

"Hey, that sounds like fun. You know it's always about community service. Give me a call next week with the details."

"I'll do that." I gave Mia another hug and walked out of the café.

As promised, Mia contacted me the next week. She gave me all the details for the community service project and party. We chatted on the phone for a couple of hours. Besides the local chapter, I learned quite a bit about Mia. Conversation flowed between us like the water that dances in front of the Bellagio Hotel in Las Vegas. Back, forth, up, down, animated, serene, playful, graceful. Our conversation was candid and relaxed. I liked talking to Mia and it was an easy decision for me to invite her to my place the following night to kick it, drink, and talk some more.

When I opened the door to greet Mia, I immediately took in her attire. She had on a dark brown suede cap that matched her eyes. Her hair, jet black with auburn highlights, hung below and on the side of the cap. She wore a red scarf tossed carelessly around her neck, a midriff brown jacket that matched the hat, faded flared denim jeans, and high-heeled dark brown suede boots. Her earrings, also brown, were big and had a gold base. Her outfit was stylish with a hint of attitude and pizzazz, yet subtlety cozy and relaxed. She looked good.

When I met Mia at the coffee shop, I did not take in her appearance. Nor did I pay any attention to her features. I focused more on the fact that she was my soror. But here, standing in my doorway, I notice that this girl is fine. Cocoa. Butter. Fine.

I looked into her eyes and noted a hint of mischief within their sparkling slant. Her nose was small and pudgy – it fit her heart-shaped face perfectly. Her lips, coated with just a trace of gloss, were full. As she smiled, I noticed straight, white teeth.

Suddenly I realized I have yet to speak to Mia as she stood patiently at the threshold of my apartment.

"Hey, girl," I said as I pulled her in for a hug.

"I was beginning to wonder if I had the right place and if you were the same girl I met last week," she said.

"My bad. I don't know what I was thinking. You look different today than when I saw you last week. Your outfit is fly! I feel a little bummy in these sweats and t-shirt."

"You look comfortable. I had a meeting with my advisor today. That's the only reason why I'm dressed up a notch. Please believe my feet are killing me in these boots!"

"Come on in and take your boots off." As Mia bent over to remove her boots I found myself staring at her incredibly plump ass.

"That's much better," she said as she straightened. She removed her scarf and jacket. Beneath the suede jacket was a casual, fitting brown t-shirt with the words "Girls Rule" in gold glitter displayed across her ample bosom. Her shirt was tucked neatly into her jeans where I noticed that her waist was tiny enough to give this girl a remarkable hour-glass figure.

"I can't remember the last time I wore heels," I said to both Mia and myself.

"I don't wear them very often. You know how we do. I'll throw them on for the occasional party, but other than that, I'm all about the gym shoes! Today, though, I really needed to make a favorable impression on my advisor."

"Why? I mean, what's going on?"

"There are so few black women in television and film. I don't mean on camera, I mean on the other side. Directing. I figured that if I went into his office dressed up a notch, he'd see that I really mean business. I am not taking my dreams lightly."

"I feel you. Do your thang, girl!"

"I'm trying."

"So what do you want to do? Are you hungry? You wanna make dinner? Wanna go out? Rent a movie? See what's on tv?"

"I'm cool just chillin'. Do you have some wine?"

"I have both red and white."

"Let's go for the red first," Mia requested.

Mia followed me into my kitchen as I went to get the wine and bottle opener. "Tell me about you," she said. "Following our conversation last night, I feel like you know quite a bit about me, but I don't know anything about you! That's not a good way to start a friendship."

She stood on the opposite side of the counter as I opened the wine. "Hmm ... well ... you already know I'm from up north and I'm in med school. Second year. I want to be a pediatrician. I have a younger brother and sister," I paused. "That's really it. I have a boring existence right now." I handed her a glass of merlot.

"That's it? Come on, soror. Tell me you dreams. Do you like to travel? What makes you laugh? What makes you cry?" She took a sip of her wine.

"That's a lot of questions."

"You think so? I think I like to analyze people too much. I need to know their inner being. How they function. Their thought process. Weird, huh?"

"No. No. It's cool," I said as I headed to the living room. I sat on the couch. "Maybe we should all analyze people more before we up and decide to call them a friend or lover. Maybe if we did that, there'd be less chaos among the masses. Maybe you should be a psychology major instead of a film studies major."

"Ha! Film studies requires a lot of analyzing." She set her glass on the coffee table before she eased herself down on the floor, next to the table, but facing me. I was somewhat amused by her ability to make herself so comfortable, so soon, in my home.

"Okay," she said. "One question at a time. What do you dream about? And I don't mean while you're sleeping!"

My first thought was to reply, "Kendall," but I quickly reeled myself in and said, "I dream about graduating and healing sick children. Sometimes I find myself wondering what my future holds, but I can't really say that I dream about the future. I just wonder. I wonder what tomorrow will bring."

"Do you like to travel?"

"I love to travel. I haven't been anywhere since I've been in college. When I was young my parents used to take me and my siblings on a different adventure every summer."

"What makes you laugh?"

I swallowed the wine I had just sipped. "Well … I find laughter in all sorts of things. Sometimes I find it in the obvious, like a funny movie. Other times I can find it in the vulgar, like when my brother lets out a silent but deadly fart. Many times, I find joy and laughter in children because they keep everything so real. I think that as a nation we should all laugh more and cry less."

"Speaking of crying … what makes you cry?"

"Funerals. Life's disappointments. Frustration. Loneliness. A broken heart." I finished my wine.

"Your heart's been broken?"

"Once."

Mia sipped the last drops of her wine then rose and went to the kitchen to get the bottle. When she came back into the living room she poured the remaining contents evenly into our glasses.

"You know," she began, "broken hearts can be healed."

"Says who?" I asked.

"I mean, I've heard that they can. I've never had a broken heart so I offer this advice with absolutely no authority."

"Mmm. I guess time will tell." We each sat silently trapped by our own thoughts. For me, thoughts of Kendall penetrated my heart and head. I had no idea what Mia was wrestling with within her mind.

"Are you hungry, Mia?" I asked. "Let's kill this deep stuff, make a salad, and feed our stomachs rather than our minds."

"Cool."

We padded back to the kitchen, drinks in hand. I opened the fridge and took out lettuce, a tomato, a cucumber, a red bell pepper, and shredded cheese. Mia rummaged through my drawers until she found a knife.

"Be careful with that thing. You've been drinking!" I chided.

"You should talk," she replied. "Say 'cheese sticks eat beaches' real fast."

"Cheese slicks eat bitches," my tongue twisted.

"Exactly! Now you tell me who's been drinking!" We both laughed.

Our salads prepared, we sat at the kitchen table and ate quietly while jazz vibrated softly throughout my apartment.

"Okay, this is gonna sound really weird, but I like being here with you," Mia said.

"What's so weird about it?"

"I don't know. It's just not very often that you meet someone, talk to them for hours during the very first telephone call, chill at their crib, have moments of silence, and still feel like everything is cool."

I didn't verbally respond to Mia. I shook my head in agreement and then got up to rinse our plates and place them in the dishwasher. I took the bottle of white wine out of the fridge and opened it. Mia rinsed our glasses before I poured the wine.

"Let's see what's on tv."

"Works for me. Just don't get upset if I start analyzing what's on. It's the film buff in me," Mia said as she followed behind me.

"It's all good. I'll even let you pick what we watch." I reached for the remote to turn off the stereo then sat down on the couch. Mia picked up the television remote and sat down on the floor again, but this time her back was against the couch and she was a mere six inches away from me. As I watched Mia flip through the channels, I felt an immense amount of heat and wondered what the hell was wrong with me.

Mia was a free spirit. A dreamer. I liked her style and her willingness to have deep conversations that went below the surface. That plus the fact that she is fine as hell. How in the world am I going to be able to maintain a friendship with this chick when non-platonic thoughts were working their way into my mind?

"Okay, chica. I can't find anything worthwhile on tv. Ain't it a shame that we pay all that money for cable and there's never a damn thing on? I have a movie in my bag that I need to watch for my Contemporary Film Theory class. Wanna watch it?"

"That's cool. What is it?"

"I don't even know. Let me get my bag." Mia got up and went to the door to retrieve her bag. Back, and again sitting on the floor, she dug around in the bag until she pulled out a dvd that had clearly been illegally dubbed.

"Hey, isn't it against the law to make copies of movies? Don't you know you could go to jail and pay a fine if you get caught with that thing? Have you ever heard the term copyright infringement?" I teased.

"I have indeed. I keep telling my professor he better lay low on the bootleg shit, but he just doesn't listen. Kinda hypocritical, huh?"

"Ya think?" I said sarcastically.

Mia read her syllabus. "This movie is called *Imagine Me and You*. It's a love story between two women. I'm supposed to parallel the modern day love story to a classic, like Romeo and Juliet."

"Oh."

"Hey, if it makes you uncomfortable, we don't have to watch it. I can watch it at home. No biggie."

"What makes you think I'm uncomfortable?"

"Does your 'oh' count?"

"If I had said 'oh' followed by a groan, then, yes, it would count. But all I said was 'oh' followed by a period."

"Was it a single period or three consecutive periods which would then indicate hesitation?"

"Would you shut up and put the damn movie in?" I nudged her with my foot.

"Okay. Okay. You don't have to get violent about it." Mia crawled to the tv, put the dvd in the dvd player, and crawled back to her spot on the floor.

Mia and I didn't say one word to each other as the movie played. We were both engrossed by the incredible love story that was unfolding on the screen. Even though the main characters were women, their love was no different than that shared between a man and a woman. When the movie was over, I was mad because I wanted the story to keep going. I found myself caught up in the happily ever after that was depicted in the movie.

"Wow. That was a good movie," Mia said.

"Yeah, it was. They made being a lesbian look easy."

"I think being a lesbian, or anybody for that matter, should always be easy. All you have to do is be true to yourself. Who cares what everyone else thinks?"

"Everybody cares what everyone else thinks. Case in point, you cared what your advisor thought about you today when you had the meeting with him."

"Yeah, but that's different."

"How?"

"Shit, I don't know. It's hard to rationalize after four glasses of wine."

"Correction. You've had five. I've had three."

"Argumentative, I see."

"I am so not argumentative. I'm just stating the facts."

"Okay. Well my five to your three. Since I drank the most, do I get a prize?" The mischievous sparkle that I saw in Mia's eyes earlier in the evening returned.

"What kind of prize?" I stared directly into her eyes, unwilling to break her stare.

"I don't know, but it sounded like a good question when it popped into my head." The sparkle in her eyes faded.

I stood up from the couch and stretched. The living room felt tense for some reason. I reached down to pick up our glasses that sat empty on the coffee table.

Mia touched my arm. "How come you haven't asked me about my love life?"

"You told me you've never had a broken heart so that led me to believe you've never been in love."

"I haven't. I've dated around. I just haven't found the one yet."

"What are you looking for?" I asked, curious.

"I'm looking for a dreamer. Someone willing to take risks and able to see past the here and now. I need a big heart and lots of attention. I need respect, trust, admiration ... love."

"That sounds like a tall order," I replied. "What are you willing to give?"

"All of the above."

"Sounds good to me. I'm sure it will happen for you."

"What about you? What are you looking for?"

"I'm not sure that I'm looking, but if I were, I'd be looking for the same as you. Maybe a little less dreaming and more just being. You know what I mean?" I asked while remembering Kendall's unwillingness to "just be" with me.

"I think so."

"One thing my last relationship taught me is you can't hide from who you are or what you want."

"Who are you, Tina?" Mia probed.

"I'm just me."

She Put It On Me

TINA

Mia and I continued to talk about life, love, and everything in between until we drifted off to sleep on my couch. She lay at one end, I lay at the other. I couldn't get comfortable. Our legs kept getting intertwined and I was afraid to stretch out because my body was very conscience of the warm body that kept brushing up against my own. After an hour or so of restless sleep, I sat up. I could hear raindrops as they gently hit the living room window. I glanced at Mia as she took short, even breaths. One day, somebody was going to be real lucky to wake up to that face each and every morning. I sighed and stood. Mia shifted and slowly opened her eyes.

"Are you okay?" she asked, her voice husky from an alcohol-induced sleep.

"I'm fine. I don't sleep well on couches."

"I'm sorry. Was I crowding you?"

"No! You're fine. Do you want a blanket or anything?"

"Sure."

I walked to the linen closet to get a blanket for Mia. When I returned, I observed that Mia had stood and was removing her jeans. Her hat was long gone as it had fallen off when we drifted to sleep. I slowly exhaled as I indulged in the vision before me. You will never witness heaven on earth until you see a beautiful, shapely girl in nothing more than panties and a cute t-shirt standing in your very own living room!

Mia caught me staring. She held my gaze as she slowly folded her jeans before placing them on the floor beside the couch. I walked towards her, blanket still in hand.

"Thanks for the blanket."

"You're welcome," I whispered as we stood facing one another with nothing more than the folded blanket between us.

She reached for the warm, thick blanket. Her fingers, soft, grazed mine. I unintentionally dropped the blanket. Our fingers interlaced causing chill bumps to consume me. I shivered.

"Are you cold?" she asked me.

"I should be asking you that." I glanced down at her sexy thighs.

She laughed softly, as did I. Then Mia, clearly the aggressor, held my face in her hands and slowly placed her lips on mine. It was a simple gesture. Nothing more than a short, sweet brushing of lips. But having not kissed a woman's lips since Kendall, there was no way in the world that I was going to let Mia get away with something as uncomplicated as a peck on the lips. So even though she withdrew her lips from mine, my face followed hers until she could not or perhaps

SHE *Slipped* AND FELL

would not retreat any further. When my lips finally caught up with hers again, I sucked on her bottom lip and then licked the top until they parted ever so slightly and allowed my tongue to meet her own.

As we kissed, my hands reached down and held Mia's juicy ass. *Dear God, am I really gripping that spectacular protrusion that was packed just right in those denim jeans*? Mia groaned and I knew that this was not a dream. It was the real deal. My hands explored every piece of exposed skin that I could reach. Her body was silky smooth.

I withdrew from our kiss and discovered the mischievous glint back in her eyes. I took Mia's hand and led her to my bedroom. Once there, I removed her shirt and was amazed to learn that the fullness of her breasts were natural. She wore no padded protection. She wore no bra. Further inspection allowed me to discover a gorgeous, multi-colored butterfly tattoo resting on the inner cleavage of her left breast. I stared at this incredibly perfect specimen named Mia and exhaled again, the second time in one night. She reached out to me and guided my head to her breasts where I rested before turning to take one of the perfectly sculptured mounds accentuated with what looked like a Hershey Kiss into my mouth. Again Mia moaned and pulled me further into her.

As I explored her, she pulled down my pants and we separated just long enough to get my shirt over my head. I dropped to my knees and rubbed my nose across her panties as I inhaled her powdery fresh scent.

My tongue pushed her panties aside and absorbed as much sweet, succulent juice as it could. Mia rubbed her clit up and down against my tongue until she couldn't take it any longer. She fell across my bed, totally relaxed. My fingers penetrated her walls and massaged her to a second explosion.

Mia rested for a while before she encouraged me to lie on my back so she could straddle me. I lay there with my toes pointed upwards, gripping Mia's waist, watching her breasts bounce up and down. Her butterfly tattoo appeared as if it were in a spasmodic flight as she rode me to my climax. Right when I reached the ultimate moment, a display of lightning flashed across my window and a crusade of thunder boomed loudly. The butterfly drifted to a halt.

Sweaty and spent, Mia lay on top of me as we both tried to catch our breath and conceptualize what had just happened.

While I didn't know what to say, I opened my mouth to speak. Mia quickly silenced me with a kiss and said, "Let's talk about this in the morning."

Morning

TINA

Morning came, but when I awoke, Mia was already gone.

"Shit." I cursed out loud. I looked around my apartment for a note, but she left none. What did that mean? Was she embarrassed? Pissed?

"Fuck." I uttered a different curse word this time as I looked at the blanket that never had the chance to cover Mia.

"Damn it." I shook my head.

Today was Saturday. The sorority community service event was this afternoon. What will I say to Mia? What was she going to say to me? Anything?

I trudged back to my room, head down and confused as I fell face first across my bed. Then I saw it. On the floor next to her panties was a piece of paper torn neatly into the shape of a heart. I reached for the note and the panties. The note read:

These are still wet. It'll probably take some time for them to dry as they got wet the moment you opened the door to let me in your apartment. I can come back for them later – if you don't mind. Thank you, Tina, for opening up to me. I enjoy your conversation, your laughter, and looking into your mysterious eyes. I think I might like to dream with you. Would you like to take a risk and "just be" with me? Mia

"Girl," I said to myself, "you don't even have to ask!"

Opening The Door
TINA

I arrived at the community center on time and was glad to see a fair number of cars already in the lot. As I rounded the corner of the parking lot, I walked head first into the chest of a very familiar smelling male. I raised my eyes and my jaw dropped in disbelief as I looked right into the eyes of Tonio.

"Tonio," I whispered.

"Tina?" he asked excitedly. I couldn't imagine why he'd be excited to see me.

"What are you doing here?"

"Helping out a friend." He pointed to a huge guy a few steps behind him. The guy had thick muscles and a neck the size of a tree trunk. He had to be a football player.

"Your friend?" I asked stupidly.

"Yeah, my friend."

I must have looked like a complete idiot as I stood there trying to digest what had just happened to me. Why in the world was my pro football-playing ex-boyfriend in Atlanta, Georgia? And why, oh why, did I have to run into him?

"Are you playing for Atlanta now?" Admittedly, I had not followed his career.

"No, I play for San Francisco. But we square off against Atlanta tomorrow night. We are always encouraged to participate in community service so here I am helping out for a few hours."

"Oh."

"I guess you haven't followed my career, huh?"

I shook my head no.

"And to think you claimed to have loved me," he said with no feeling, but with piercing eyes.

"I did."

"Right. And I guess that's why you dumped me? Or was the dick simply not good enough for you? Kendall offered something more appealing?" He smirked and the mole just above the left corner of his lip was suddenly hidden in facial wrinkles.

"How did you know about Kendall?"

"Come on, Tina. I was physically gone from the campus, but I still had a lot of friends there. They couldn't wait to tell me how my ex-girl was licking the coochie. They kept me well informed," he said with venom oozing from his voice.

I turned to walk back towards my car.

"Aren't you going to say something, Tina?"

I shook my head no and quickened my pace.

"Tina!" he yelled. "Tina!"

I thought I heard him running to catch up with me. I didn't turn around to see. I quickly unlocked my car, got in, locked the doors, started the ignition, backed out the parking space, and sped away. Undergrad,

Tonio, Kendall – that was a closed chapter in my life and that's the way I intended to keep it.

I drove aimlessly around I-285 two complete times before I realized I had nowhere to go and not nearly enough gas to get there! How could a day full of such potential turn out to be so bad? Of all the places for me to bump into Tonio, why here? Why today?

And what was Mia thinking? Was she angry? I needed to call her and explain why I didn't show up today. I hurriedly pulled into a parking spot in front of my apartment with the intent to call Mia, but I was immediately sidetracked as I saw Laz sitting on the steps outside my door. Great. What else can happen today?

Lazarus looked ill. I walked toward him and in a sudden flurry he broke out with a confession about how much he missed the ranch in Oklahoma. He informed me that he had dropped out of med school and was moving back home. Lazarus was truly a black cowboy and I never thought he really fit in at Unity anyway.

"Tina, I'm so sorry to do this to you. I should have been more open with you and shared my feelings of discontent instead of springing news of my departure on you like this."

"You're damn right! Lazarus, how could you do this to me? To us?" I played the role of a bitter, desolate girlfriend.

"I'm sorry. But we can still be together. We can visit each other, write, call, e-mail. I'm willing to do whatever it takes for us to stay together."

"No, I'm not into the long distance thing," I said as I bowed out of the opportunity to continue a relationship that didn't have any meaning for me in the first place.

As Lazarus walked away, I watched his awkward stride before I entered my apartment. I sat on my couch and leaned my head back. Whenever I look back and remember life in undergrad, emotions overcome me that I can't identify. Feelings arise that tug at my heart and confuse the hell out of me. In particular, my feelings for Kendall are the most perplexing.

I love Kendall. First, I love her as a friend. When we were "just friends" life was good. She was like a sister to me. We did things that sisters do: shop, party, watch tv, talk about men. Damn it, we were regular!

But I also love her as a companion. Though I never originally thought of her as a potential sex partner or someone to lust after, it became very easy to do. Kendall is beautiful. Plus she's quiet and well respected. She's smart. She has a killer smile. It wasn't until she literally fell on top of me that I became alarmingly aware of just how beautiful she is. Her eyebrows are naturally arched. Her skin radiates when she smiles. Her cheekbones are high, her dimples are deep, and her lips are full. Her light-brown eyes are astonishing because up close, I discovered they contain little gold flecks that sparkled in the light. And then, her hair. Kendall's hair is smooth and though she wears it in a bob, her hair sometimes covers her right eye giving her a look of innocence.

I miss her. I miss our talks and the silly things we would do in order to amuse ourselves.

Okay, I could deal with the fact that I missed my friend. And even my lover. But the more frustrating thing for me is that thinking about Kendall seems to open up a deep, deep door in the back of my mind where hidden feelings of female attractions are secretly kept, locked away. I can recall having a crush on my babysitter when I was young. Like five or six years young! As a matter of fact, I've had countless crushes on female classmates over the years. But I never did anything about them. And as I've grown older and watched movies, I've become increasingly aware of the naked female body and the intense reaction it has in my pubic region.

From a very early age, I always knew females were not supposed to like females. It wasn't anything my parents sat me down and told me. It was just a child's observation. From the story of Adam and Eve, Mr. and Mrs. Claus, Mom and Dad, to people I saw in public – I was cognizant enough to detect female-female or male-male relationships simply were not the norm. But not even my understanding at age five of what the public found acceptable could take away my perception of beauty and what I personally am attracted to.

In grade school, I occasionally heard the words "faggot" or "funny" and instantly made the connection between these degrading words and a male who wasn't masculine.

In junior high school I heard the words "homosexual" and "gay" and the meaning behind them. Likewise, I began to hear the phrase, "The Bible says …" Everything I heard and saw pointed to no. No, two men or two women could not be in a relationship. No, two people of the same sex could not love another. No, two people with the same body parts could not please one another. No, God does not condone homosexuality.

Yet, even in my understanding of public opinion, no one could tell me why these things were forbidden. Why couldn't two people of the same sex be in a relationship, love one another, or have sex? Why? I never voiced my questions and I never shared my aching desire to kiss a woman's lips, suck upon her breasts, or have her legs wrapped around me.

In high school, I simply pushed all my feelings back into the corner of my mind, behind the closed door, and lived my life. And while I didn't stare at my friends' bodies as we dressed and undressed in the girls' locker room, I was still very much in tune with my likes and dislikes in regard to the female population. I knew what I found attractive, be it male or female. I liked masculinity in a male and femininity in a female.

My college years were so wrapped around Tonio, I didn't have the opportunity to open the locked door in my head very often until the night Kendall slipped and fell on top of me. My silence that night was not based on anger or even confusion. Instead it was like my secret, closed door was suddenly forcibly opened and I couldn't run or hide from the buried feelings that were behind the door anymore.

I'll admit that since I've been at Unity, I'm more likely to look at a woman and swallow her image. Along those same lines, as I walk the campus or the village, I always try to meet the eyes of a woman that I am attracted to just to see if she'll acknowledge my interest. To date, no one has. At least, not in a way I can decipher. I'm new to this game and I don't know how to break the barrier and let these females know I'm interested. Now, with absolutely no warning, Mia pops into my life. I know that I like her. I'm very much attracted to her. I also know that I still love Kendall. I miss her. If I hadn't have been so stubborn, maybe she'd still have been a part of my life.

As for Tonio and Laz, they were a serious attempt on my part to be like the world thinks I should be. Yet I know that I can never be happy with a male partner. Nor do I receive satisfaction from anything male. I love ladies. I desire women. I am a lesbian.

The Club

TINA

The sound of the telephone ringing penetrated my sleep. Just as soon as it began, it stopped. Then, it rang again.

"Hello," I mumbled. No one said anything. I hung up.

The phone rang again. "Hello," I said as I sat up. This time I was wide awake.

"Dyke!" I recognized Tonio's voice. I hung up and tried not to be mad. The phone rang again.

"What?" I yelled, unable to control my anger.

"Are you upset with me?" Mia's voice cautiously posed the question. "I know I left your place early. I had to get home and get things ready for the kids today. You looked so peaceful as you slept, I didn't have the heart to wake you. I thought the note said it all …" her voice trailed off.

"Mia, no, I'm not mad at you." How interesting that she thought I was upset with her. She hadn't done anything wrong. I'm the one who failed to help out with the service project. "I should have called you. I had a really crazy day today. I thought about you and the connection that took place last night. I wanted to call, but when I didn't show up for the service project I thought you would be upset with me."

"I wondered where you were ..."

"I've been home. Thinking. Getting to know me."

"I'd like to get to know you, too, Tina."

"I'd say that after last night you're off to a very good start."

"Let's go have some fun tonight. I sense that you need to be in an atmosphere where you can just be. I know just the place. Get your party clothes on. I'll be there in thirty."

"I don't have any party clothes," I replied as I mentally examined my wardrobe. I hadn't gone out to a club or a party since undergrad. It didn't matter. Mia had already hung up the phone.

"I haven't partied in over a year," I said to myself as I headed to my closet to try and find a sexy, fashionable outfit.

Mia arrived at my door exactly thirty minutes later. I had just added the finishing touches to my hair and sprayed some oil sheen on it to add optimum shine. I opened the door when I heard the doorbell and my jaw dropped to the floor when I saw Mia standing there looking fine as hell. For real. Her hair was pinned up with a few strands falling teasingly in her face. Her short, black leather jacket was unzipped and revealed a black and silver bustier that showed all kinds of cleavage. I must be a breast woman 'cause I couldn't stop staring at her voluptuous mounds of firm flesh just waiting for me to take a lick. She had on fitting black jeans and a silver chain belt. Black high-heeled boots and silver jewelry topped off the outfit.

"Damn! You look good!"

"I tried to put something together that might turn you on," she smiled.

"Mission accomplished."

"You ready?"

"Yeah."

Mia drove us to a gay and lesbian club off MLK Avenue. The place was dimly lit. There was a stage and a dance floor. This was the first time I had ever been in a gay and lesbian club. I loved it. Here, there were no pretenses. It was okay for me to hold hands with Mia. No one looked at me like I was a leper.

There was no place to sit and have intimate conversation. Instead, patrons were expected to let the music pulse through their bodies and simply let go and escape the outside world.

Mia and I danced together which was something I never got to do with Kendall. As we danced I watched her butterfly tattoo flutter and move to the beat that flowed within Mia. We touched. We kissed. And here, it was okay.

"Are you thirsty?" I half spoke half yelled to Mia.

"Yeah."

"Want a beer?"

"Yes, please."

I left the dance floor to get our ice cold drinks. As I waited my turn at the bar, I scanned the crowd and observed singles and couples just out to have a good time.

My eyes ultimately zoned in on Mia though. The dj was playing the music for a shuffle that I did not know. If it wasn't the Electric Slide, I couldn't do it. But Mia … Mia knew the dance and she was on the dance floor doing her thang. She had long lost the leather jacket. It was too hot in the club to wear it. Even from the bar I could see a thin layer of sweat on her face, arms, and abs.

A guy bumped into her as he shuffled in the wrong direction. He and Mia giggled, but she didn't let his misstep disturb her groove. I ordered our beers just as the song ended. As I walked back to Mia, I noticed a tall, attractive, masculine-looking female say something to Mia. Mia shook her head no and pointed at me. The woman sauntered away, but not before I heard her mumble, "Damn, lipstick lesbians." I didn't know what she meant, but it really didn't matter because Mia was walking towards me.

"I missed you," she whispered in my ear. I smiled, took a sip of my beer and wiped the moisture from her arm.

"Thank you for bringing me here."

Femmes And Studs

TINA

Mia took me to Waffle House after we left the club. There's nothing like a good greasy meal, breakfast in particular, after a night of drinking and dancing.

We were waiting for our order when Mia asked, "Was it a girl that broke your heart?"

"Yes. My first. We didn't know how to openly love one another. We were caught up in trying to figure out who we were, what we wanted, and how to define and accept the reality of our relationship."

"Are you still friends?"

"I haven't spoken to her since the break up."

The waitress brought our drinks. "What's her name?"

"Kendall."

"Are you still in love with her?"

I hesitated before answering, "Sometimes I think I am."

Mia sipped her orange juice. "I didn't peg you as a lesbian when we met in the coffee shop."

"You know, I've been a lesbian my entire life. But I don't think I fully accepted it until I met you. I've been trying so hard to be regular, but what I've found is that being regular doesn't make me happy." I smiled. "And for the record, I didn't think you were a lesbian, either. I just viewed you as a soror."

"It's funny, huh? You can spend your whole life searching for normalcy when, really, there's no such thing."

"For the longest time, I thought my attraction to women was a defect in my makeup. Believe me, I tried so hard to be like everybody else. But I think the older I get, the more difficult it becomes. When Kendall and I hooked up, it felt so natural to me. So right. But the difficulty in being out was too much for Kendall. And me, too, I think. Then, down here at Unity, I tried to revert back to society's definition of normal, but believe me when I tell you I found no joy in it. Then you came along and I just want to chill and do me for once. You know? The thing of it is, I don't even know how to be a lesbian. I don't know if there are certain rules I'm supposed to follow. I know nothing."

"You don't have to know anything. All you have to do, Tina, is be yourself. We can sit down and talk about the intricacies, the roles that some folks get stuck on, but the bottom line is to be yourself and like whatever you're attracted to."

"That chick at the club that you declined a dance called us lipstick lesbians as she walked away. What's a lipstick lesbian?" I asked, assuming Mia would know.

Mia laughed. "By all accounts, we are. Lipstick lesbians are feminine women, or femmes. In the lesbian world, most relationships involve a femme and a stud which is a more masculine, aggressive female. Occasionally, you'll see femme couples. Very rarely will you see two studs together."

"Okay. I get it. So we're femmes. Right. When I see myself with a woman, I don't envision me with a stud. My woman is always sexy and very feminine. Is that okay?"

"Sweetie, you like what you like. Don't ever let society tell you what you can and can't have. I like feminine women, too. I'm not attracted to masculine women at all. But that's just me. And apparently you, too. As our relationship grows, assuming we develop a relationship, it will be very interesting to see who is the more dominant one in our relationship."

"Dominant how so?"

"The aggressor. All relationships, male-female, female-female, and male-male, have a more aggressive partner. It's human nature. It's usually just the stronger of the two. It doesn't mean one person will call all the shots. It could be that where one is strong, the other is weak and vice versa. It means I'll hold you up when you need to lean or you'll carry me over the water when the water is too deep for me to wade through."

"Are you sure you're not a psychology major?"

"Positive. It's just what I've learned. It's the psychology of life."

"When did you experience your first relationship with a female?"

"I had my first in high school. I've always known I was a lesbian. I've never been with a guy. I wouldn't know what to do with a man even if he came with a diagram. I have no desire to lay down with a man or to allow him to invade me. The thought makes me shiver. Tons of men have hit on me, but I've never, ever been interested."

"I can honestly say that being with a man does not compare to being with a woman."

"I'm not surprised. To each his own, that's my motto. It drives my family crazy."

"So your family knows? They know you date women?"

"It would be very amazing for them not to know seeing how I've never had a boyfriend!" Mia smiled. "I told my parents I liked girls when I was in elementary school. They said it was a phase. I told them again when I was in middle school. They said I'd grow out of it. When they caught me and my best friend making out in the basement, they suddenly realized that maybe there was a little more to what I had been trying to tell them.

"My dad was okay with it. He said just make sure the girl is pretty. My mom had a much more difficult time with it. She still thinks I'll grow out of it. I try to tell her that you don't grow out of being homosexual. It's not a choice. But she doesn't understand. I even went through counseling per her request. It didn't change who I am or how I feel."

"So you're completely out. I mean people on campus know that you date women?"

"I'm as out as I know how to be. I don't tell each and every person I meet that I'm a lesbian. My sexual orientation is irrelevant in so much of my day-to-day existence. But if you ask me, I will tell you. And I don't have a problem with letting people know."

"That's amazing." The waitress set our plates in front of us. "When I think about telling my family, my stomach hurts. I don't know how they'll react. But when I think about keeping it to myself, my stomach hurts even more. I don't want to live my life behind closed doors anymore.

"Tonight was so incredible for me. To be in a gay club and to see other people like myself. Damn. It just felt so good! Before tonight I'd never been in a gay club!"

"I'm glad to be the one to open your mind and spread your horizons. I'm happy to be the first woman you've been 'out' with. There's so much more for you to learn."

"Will you show me? Teach me?"

"If you allow me to."

The Folks

TINA

I did. I allowed Mia to teach me and show me what it meant to love myself, and her, as a lesbian. While trying hard not to neglect my studies, I spent every waking moment doing all things homosexual. I went to the clubs. I went to drag shows. I found out where the gay and lesbian districts were in the city. I attended a pride event. I discovered rainbows.

I experienced disgust-filled stares on campus and in the city when Mia and I walked, lost completely in each other, holding hands and displaying subtle affection. But I didn't care. I just wanted to live my life as a woman who happened to be in love with another woman.

Love. Did I really love Mia? Or did I love the education that Mia was giving me? I hadn't fully answered the question when Mia decided she wanted to take me home to meet her parents.

"Come on, baby. It's Christmas. You can't spend the day stuck up in your apartment! I know you want a good, home-cooked Christmas dinner."

SHONDA

Mia was right. Nicole and Miguel had left the city for the holidays. Since money was tight, I opted not to go home over the break. Mia's family lived right here in the city. I couldn't think of one good reason not to have dinner with her and her parents. Unless, of course, you count the fact that I was scared as hell.

"Okay. I'll go."

"Excellent," Mia said as she laid a kiss on my lips.

The drive to her parents' house only took twenty minutes. Funny, huh? I'm starting to sound like a true Atlanta native with the twenty-minute thing! We had been dating for a year and this was the first time I had ventured to meet the parents. Being out among strangers is one thing, being out with family is different. Don't ask me why, it just is.

"Mom. Dad. I'm home!" Mia said as she walked in to her childhood home.

"Well alright. My baby girl is here. Merry Christmas," a tall, muscular, graying gentleman said as he embraced his daughter. It was clear that Mia's genes jumped straight out of her father and into her.

"Hey, Daddy. Merry Christmas." Mia hugged her father. "This is Tina." Mia reached for my hand, but I didn't know if it was okay to hold her hand in front of her parents. I hesitated. It was a good thing I paused because in walked her mother.

"Merry Christmas, Mia." She hugged her daughter, but kept her eyes on me.

"Merry Christmas, Mom. This is Tina."

Her mother eyed me up and down, left and right. I felt naked even though I had on tailored dress pants and a sweater.

"Pleased to meet you." Mia's father pulled me in for a bear hug. "We've heard quite a lot about you."

"Welcome," Mia's mother said in a very dry and matter-of-fact tone. I glanced at Mia. She winked at me and I tried my damnedest to relax.

But relaxation did not come easy thanks to frequent stares from Mia's mother. We were at the dinner table with a feast of ham, greens, sweet potatoes, rolls, green beans, macaroni and cheese, chocolate cake, sweet potato pie, and fruit punch waiting to be devoured. The meal smelled delectable and I couldn't wait to dig in as evidenced by my growling stomach. Yet I was so nervous, I couldn't even pick up my fork.

"Thanks for allowing me to share Christmas dinner with your family," I said to Mia's parents.

"You are welcome any time," Mia's father responded.

"I have to admit, you're a pretty lesbian," Mia's mother commented.

I didn't know how to respond. I looked at Mia for help.

"Mom. Was that really necessary?" Mia chided her mother.

"She is pretty," Mia's mother said as if I weren't sitting across from her. "We never get to meet your girlfriends. I had no idea that you dated pretty women. I thought that since you're attractive, you would date a woman that looks like a man."

Mia's mouth dropped. I totally froze. I mean, what could I possibly say?

"Wow. This makes for interesting table talk," Mia's father interjected. "Tina, my apologies to you on behalf of my wife. She means no disrespect." He glanced sternly at his wife. "We've known for years that our daughter likes and dates women. But we've never had the opportunity to meet someone she is dating. You, my dear, are the first. We are, admittedly, ignorant on this topic. We always assumed that she'd date a masculine woman. We are somewhat astounded by your beauty yet, delightfully, honored that our daughter has met someone that she could bring home."

"Umm. Okay." Way to go, Tina. That was a real intelligent response. I took a deep breath.

Mia reached for my hand under the table. I exhaled. "Not only is she beautiful, she's smart, too." Mia complimented me as she squeezed my hand. Rather than say something stupid, I remained silent.

"Can she cook?" her mom asked as she took a bite of her own homemade roll.

"Probably not nearly as well as you." I finally found my voice.

"If we see your face around here more often I might teach you, both of you, a thing or two," her mom said, this time taking a bite of greens.

We got over the hurdle. Even though her parents didn't know me, they were willing to take a chance and get to know me. I tasted the food on my plate, which was delicious, and realized I was willing to get to know them as well.

Differences
TINA

While Mia was willing to be open about me with her family, my lack of willingness to be open with my family caused stress in our relationship. Even though my family was way up north, Mia took it as a slight when I failed to acknowledge our relationship to my folks.

"So I'm good enough to sleep with, but I'm not good enough to tell your family about? Am I too low class? Too free about who I am? Maybe I'm too hood? Is that it?"

"Mia, no. I'm just not ready to share this with them yet. I definitely don't want to do it over the phone."

"Uh-huh. I'm tired of you referring to me as just a friend when they call. I feel like a dirty little secret."

"You and I both know that you're not my dirty little secret. Mia, I love you!"

"I can't tell."

And so the argument would go. We never resolved it. We just let it die. Until the next time.

SHONDA

My beef with Mia was with her so-called "friends." Mia maintained contact with her exes. And even though the relationships were supposedly over, that didn't stop the occasional phone call or text message that contained inappropriate – in my mind – contact.

"If y'all are just friends, then why is she sending you messages with vivid details about what she'd like to do to you, Mia?"

"She doesn't mean anything by it. She's just messing around. We're just friends."

"Friends my chocolate-coated ass! It is disrespectful for her to be calling during the hours she calls, to be texting the bullshit texts that she sends, and to e-mail you like y'all are still down for one another. It's even more disrespectful for you to allow this bullshit behavior to continue!"

"Kinda like it's disrespectful of you not to tell your parents about us. Right, Tina?"

"Whatever. I can't sleep with my parents."

"I'm not gonna sleep with my exes!"

"Of course not. You'd rather have an emotional affair with them instead. You make me sick!"

"You are a closeted coward!"

We had countless arguments similar to this one. She was hurt by my inability to come out to my parents. I was hurt by her continued relationships with her exes. It finally got to the point where the arguments were getting way out of hand. We were hurting each other, when what we should have done was listen to what the other had to say and how the other felt. No longer wanting the name-calling and deceit to continue, I told my mom, during a telephone call, that I was dating a woman.

"You mean you're really good friends." She tried to clarify what I had told her.

"Mia is my friend, but she's also my lover. We're dating," I said as I glanced at Mia who was present while I had this conversation with my mom.

"Tina, don't let a failed relationship with a man force you to look down the other path," my mom said with all the ignorance of a person who knew nothing about the struggle of being homosexual.

"What are you talking about?"

"Tonio, dear. I'm talking about Tonio."

"This has nothing to do with Tonio! Mom, I've always been attracted to women. I just didn't know what to do about it," I said, wishing that I was having this conversation face-to-face with my mom instead of long distance.

"It's a phase, Tina. It'll pass."

"No, Mom. It's not a phase. It's a reality. It's not going to go away no matter how much you or anyone else wishes it would. I know. I've already tried."

"I can't deal with this right now. I'll talk to you later." Click. All I heard was the dial tone.

"What did she say?" Mia asked.

"She doesn't want to talk to me right now."

"You should have told her that we've been dating for over a year."

"You know what? I don't need a fuckin' after-the-fact script. I've done what you needed me to do even though I wasn't ready and it's not the manner that I wanted to do it. Now it's your turn. What the hell are you going to do?"

Fed Up With the Lies and Alibis
TINA

Nothing. She did absolutely nothing. She would go out with her exes and I'd find out about it afterwards. They called her. She'd call back. They'd text her. She'd reply. They'd e-mail her. She'd e-mail them.

She told me contact had stopped. I learned otherwise. I found her cell phone bill. I checked her e-mail. I became a possessive freak. I felt weak for her. I couldn't trust her. I told her so.

"You're such a fucking liar, Mia. You don't give a damn about me or how I feel."

"Yes, I do. It's just..."

"It's just what?"

"I have a problem."

"No shit. It's called I'm-a-fucking-liar. Dishonesty. You reek of it. And I'm sick of it."

"They don't want me."

"They can have you. Let somebody else put up with this bullshit."

"You don't mean that."

"Yeah, baby girl, I do. I don't need the drama."

Of course, my words never seemed to stick. We'd go a day, maybe two, without speaking. Then she'd call or I'd call just to see how the other was doing. Eventually we'd say how much we missed one another. Then someone would go to the other's apartment. We'd kiss. We'd make up. Everything would be good until her phone rang or she'd get a text. And I'd say who is that? 'Cause at this point I'm completely insecure and don't believe a damn thing that she says.

"It's so and so," she'd say. And I'd know within every inch of my being that she was lying. It took me a while to accept the fact that she wasn't going to change. Once a liar, always a liar. And the bad part is that once lies enter a relationship, it's hard to trust and see past all the deceit. Now, two years later, I understand why Mia's heart has never been broken. For a chick to have so much knowledge about being in the life, she lacked total knowledge when it came to fully understanding what it takes to be in a committed relationship. There was no room in my life for a liar, no matter how beautiful she may be.

Life and Death

KENDALL

I sensed something was wrong the moment I pulled into the driveway of my parents' home. Though there was nothing physically or visibly out of place, something deep down in the pit of my stomach screamed "danger!"

I pulled my car all the way up to the detached garage as I did each evening when I got home from work. The sun was setting and the sky was tinted a beautiful pink color. As I approached the side door of my parents' two-story home, I heard what sounded like a muffled cry. My pace quickened until I was directly in front of the door. Once there, I discovered the door was not fully shut. My stomach grew nervous as I pushed the door open with my foot. The door squeaked as it always did and again, I heard a muffled cry. I ran up the two steps into the kitchen and saw my father lying motionless on the kitchen floor. As I stepped closer to him, thinking that he had fallen and needed help getting up, I saw that his throat was cut open and a pool of blood surrounded his head. I covered my mouth as vomit forced its way from the lining of my stomach. I tried not to scream as I sank down beside my father, rubbed his balding head, and stared at his lifeless eyes.

"Oh, Daddy," I cried. I heard a shuffling noise coming from upstairs. I sprang up from beside my father. I grabbed a knife from the counter and began the search for my mama. The house was eerily silent and I could hear my heart beating in my ears. I reached my bedroom. The door was closed, but light filtered from the crack at the bottom.

"Mama?" I yelled as I pushed the door open.

She looked like a disheveled rag doll. She lay spread-eagle on my bed. Her blouse was torn open and her skirt was pushed up to her waist. Her panties were ripped and pulled down to her knees. I hurried into the room and felt faint when I saw the multiple stab wounds in her abdomen. I fell to the side of the bed and screamed, "Mama!"

I didn't hear him walk up behind me, but I smelled him. He smelled musty and damp. As I lifted myself from the floor and turned around to face the murderer of my parents, I was greeted with a bone-splitting pain across the bridge of my nose and left cheekbone. I never saw my attacker nor did I feel any additional pain as he raped me, stabbed me and left me for dead.

When I awoke almost eight weeks later, my face felt frozen. And my chest hurt right above my heart. I would later learn that he stabbed me three times – each time missing my heart and nearby arteries.

The doctors said I'd need plastic surgery on my face where the bookend he used to hit me with crushed my left jawbone.

The doctors also said I'd have to go through physical therapy to get my left arm strong again. The muscles and tendons he severed with the knife would take a full year to mend.

The doctors informed me that both my parents had died. They didn't need to tell me that. The vivid images of their bloodied bodies would forever be etched in my mind.

Then the doctors told me I was carrying my attacker's child.

"Take it out! Take it out! Take it out!" I yelled as loudly as I could. But my jawbone was wired shut and my vocal chords had not been used in quite some time, so the only thing that came out of my mouth was a mere whisper.

How could I be pregnant? What vile man would do something so cruel and heartless? How could he degrade me like this? Why?

After what seemed like an eternity of questions racing through my head, I tried my best to ask the doctors, "Did they catch him? Is he in jail?"

"Miss Long, there's a police officer outside your room waiting to talk to you."

I nodded my head in understanding and motioned that it was alright for the officer to come in. The doctor went to the door and spoke to the officer. The officer entered my hospital room. He was young, maybe twenty-eight, thirty max. He was black and not particularly handsome. But, then, I don't think I'll ever view men in the same manner that I once did.

"Miss Long, I'm Detective Radcliff. How are you feeling?"

I looked at the officer as if he were the dumbest, and I do mean numero uno, ass man in the world. How did he think I felt? My parents were dead. My face and body were jacked up. And there was a bastard child growing inside me.

"Uh, yes. Sorry." He cleared his throat. "Miss Long, we haven't caught your attacker. He didn't leave much for us to go on. No fingerprints. We have semen that we obtained from the body of your mother and a few pubic hairs. We have a bloody footprint casing which enables us to approximate his height. But that's all we have. Nothing we collected matches anything in our database. What we need is a description. What did he look like? What did you see?"

"I didn't see anything," I said through clenched and wired teeth. The words were unintelligible. So I just shook my head no.

"An item of clothing? A piece of jewelry?"

I tried to remember, but I kept coming up blank. Nothing. Again, I shook my head no.

"Well, here's my card. If you remember anything at all, give me a call. Day or night, it doesn't matter. What this man did to you and your family was horrible. I want him to pay. I will not close this case until justice has been served." Detective Radcliff stared deep into my eyes to make sure I knew he meant business. Then he left.

Family. I no longer had a family. My parents were dead. They died senseless, horrific deaths. No family now. Suddenly, I felt the urge to vomit. I didn't have time to lean over and throw up to the side of my bed. The way my body, and especially my face, felt, I wouldn't have been able to lean over anyway. Instead, the vomit shot out between the wires in my mouth and through my nose like a ball shoots from a cannon. A perfect arch. Most of it landed on my stomach. Instinctively my right hand tried to wipe the vomit from my hospital gown. As I rubbed my stomach, I remembered the baby. I froze. The baby growing inside me was a part of me. It was family. It was the only family I had left. I thought this as I choked on the vomit that was trapped in my nose. I couldn't breathe. The monitor beside my bed started ringing a loud, obtrusive sound. The last thing I saw before I blacked out was several nurses running into the room.

It, Him, Them, Me,

KENDALL

The fetus developing within my womb… is a part of me. It is real. But it came from him.

I did not see him. I did not hear him. I did not feel him. I did not taste him. I do not know him. I … hate … him.

It had no role in this debacle. It is faultless. It is life.

He is bad. He is evil.

It is pure. It can be molded. It can be taught. My blood runs through it.

"Good afternoon, Miss Long. Are you hungry?" My thoughts were interrupted by the nurse who brought me my nutritious, yet blended, lunch. She set the tray in front of me. Pureed chicken. Applesauce. Milk. Everything could be sipped through a straw. Nothing looked worthy of being sipped. I had no desire to eat, but my stomach felt hungry. Only eight weeks into this and it already had an appetite.

I bypassed the chicken puree and instead opted to drink the applesauce. As I sucked the grainy fruit blend, the nurse checked my blood pressure. She shook her head after she got the reading. High. My blood pressure is high. It's been high ever since I woke up in here and they told me my parents are dead and it is growing inside me.

The nurse wrote something down on my chart before she left my room. I slurped the last of the applesauce and looked out the window. My face and chest hurt. The low doses of the pain killer they had been giving me through the I.V. were not working. If I decide not to keep it, I can have stronger drugs. If I keep it, they'll give me just enough meds to keep me comfortable and it safe. The clock is ticking and I have to make a decision soon.

They reluctantly let me look in a mirror. No more high cheekbones. My face is disfigured. I look like a monster. They said the swelling will go down. I am having a difficult time believing them.

My left arm and hand don't work like they used to. They said I have to learn how to use them again.

So here I lay. Captive to them. Pregnant. Ugly. Angry. Restricted. Alone.

Night Terrors
KENDALL

The house is dark. A musty odor has permeated the walls. I can't see any windows. I can't find a door that will open and lead me out of the house. I run down the never-ending hallway as fast as I can; I can hear him behind me. He's not running. He's walking. I can feel my heart beating in my throat. I gotta run faster. I have to get out of here. Where's the doorway out?

I finally find a doorknob that turns. I open the door and realize it is my bedroom. I shut the door behind me, lock it, and slump against it. There's no time to rest. I can't hear his footsteps anymore. I push the dresser in front of the door to keep him out.

I run to the window and kick the glass until it shatters. It's a long way down, but it's the only way out. I turn around to look at the barricaded door and am startled to see my parents sitting on the dresser. I want to run to them, but as I move towards them, they begin to fade away.

I look back to the window and place my foot on the ledge. I close my eyes and take a deep breath. I jump.

I'm falling. Falling. Down I go. It is taking me a long time to reach the ground. I open my eyes and realize the house is really a skyscraper. I can feel my body accelerating as I spiral downward. I see him standing below, braced to catch me. I can't see his face, but I know it's him. I can't break my fall and go back up. I'm trapped. I try to scream, but no noise comes out. He opens his arms wider. My body collides with his.

The collision jolts me awake and I discover that I am drenched in sweat. My heart is racing. As my eyes adjust to the darkness of the hospital room, I accept that it was just a dream, another tumultuous dream from which there does not seem to be an escape.

My body trembles and tears leak from the corners of my eyes. *I can't do this. I can't live this way. Somebody please help me. Please.*

Therapy
KENDALL

"You can do it, Kendall. Push the water back, behind you," the physical therapist instructed.

"I'm trying." The wires in my mouth were removed prior to my transfer to the rehab facility.

"You can. It's mind over matter. The water is not heavy. Try."

Again I stretched both arms in front of me and then, slowly, pulled them to my side, parallel to the water's surface. The effort sent miniature ripples across the pool. Thirty minutes of this routine had left me exhausted and cranky.

"You did good today. I'll see you in a couple of days. Same time. Same place."

I exited the pool and walked towards the locker room to change out of my wet bathing suit. In front of the mirror I stole a glance at my ever-growing and protruding stomach. It seemed to grow bigger and bigger each day.

The warm spray of the shower felt good on my achy body. I lathered and rinsed. I had no desire to stand under the water, exposed, for longer than necessary. Out and dried, I put on my sweats. Everything I did felt mechanical.

Dressed, I headed to my room. I had thirty minutes to waste before the psychiatrist arrived and my session with her would begin.

I felt it kick and position itself on my right side. Two more months then it would be here.

My tastebuds had a sudden yearning for a lemon. With salt. I turned in the opposite direction of my room and headed towards the cafeteria. I passed various rehab residents all with varying degrees of deformity, but I didn't speak to any of them. They were not my friends. They could not be trusted.

I asked the cafeteria lady for a lemon. She gave me a knowing smile and said something about pregnancy cravings as she sliced the yellow fruit. She placed the lemon wedges on a plate and handed it to me. I took it from her, but I did not return her smile.

I sat down at a table and dumped salt on my lemon. My cheeks drew in as I sucked the sour juice. As I swallowed, it did somersaults in my stomach. It was like me. It liked fruit.

Time

KENDALL

"How do you feel today?"

"The same way I felt the first time you asked me that exact same question. Angry. Tired. Confused. Hurt. Maybe you'll understand me better now that my mouth isn't wired shut, eh?"

She ignored my smart comment. "Why do you feel that way?"

"Why the hell do you think?"

"How can I help you?"

"You can find the bastard who did this to me and cut his dick off. You can bring my parents back to life. You can make the nightmares stop. Or, you can just leave me the fuck alone."

"I can't do any of those things."

"Then that makes you worthless to me and I see no reason for us to continue these conversations."

"You're making such wonderful progress. Physically, your arm movement is getting better. The tendons are healing. Your jaw is healing."

"Yeah, doc, but those things have nothing to do with you. Physical therapy is healing the arm. Plastic surgery fixed the jaw. What have you done for me?"

"I'm here to listen."

What does she want to hear? How many times must I tell her how angry I am? How is talking to her helping me?

"Look, doc, I've already told you how I feel."

"Yes, but you don't feel better yet. Your feelings aren't progressing towards the positive."

"Am I supposed to feel better just because I talk to you? I don't know you like that! You don't know me! You just know my situation. You don't give a damn about me and talking to you is not going to ease my pain."

"Time will heal your pain. And so will talking. Don't hold your feelings in."

"Time, huh? I once heard that when you're dying or watching a loved one die, time is the one thing you wish you had more of. Right now, I have nothing but time. I find myself watching time go by, slowly, each and every day.

"I don't feel like I'm healing, doc. I feel like I'm dying. Time? Time is the last thing I want more of."

A Reason To Love
KENDALL

"On three I want you to push. One. Two. Three."

The epidural they gave me significantly dimmed the pain I felt with each contraction when labor first began. Now that the epidural is wearing off, I can feel an obscene amount of pressure below my waistline and I can't help but wonder why in the hell women do this.

I pushed as the doctor instructed, but it was hard for me to gauge the effectiveness of my push. If I were not doing this alone, if I had a partner beside me to coach and guide me, I imagine this would be the time when I would look to my significant other and try to determine whether my pushing is showing results or if it is all in vain. If I had a partner beside me, I might even fake a smile and act like this shit is fun.

"Very good. Take a deep breath and relax."

Relax? Who relaxes when their shit is spread wide open for all to see and it feels like the Incredible Hulk just got angry in your coochie?

I felt pressure again. "Push, Kendall."

I could feel sweat dripping down my face. I held on to the bed rail with my right hand. My left hand still wasn't strong enough to squeeze anything.

"I see a head."

Oh my God. Oh my God.

"Push."

Pop. I heard a sound very similar to a bubble busting as its head emerged from my coochie. I guess its body slid out after the popping sound, but I didn't feel it come out.

"Suction."

I heard it cry. "You have a baby girl."

Why am I crying? Why the fuck am I crying? The doctor placed it in my good arm.

My breath caught in my throat as I stared. It had a head full of black hair and glistening eyes that gazed fixedly at me. It was no longer illusory or fanciful. Her innocent presence overwhelmed my soul and I knew beyond a shadow of a doubt that I could survive this horrific ordeal because now I have a reason to live again.

I placed a tenderhearted kiss on her tiny, puckered, pink lips. This … is … my daughter.

Her

TINA

"Hey, Mama. What's going on up that way?"

"We are buried in with three feet of snow," Mama replied disgustedly.

"But it's the end of April."

"And?"

"Dang! So sorry for y'all. It's about seventy-five degrees down here in Atlanta. The sun is shining, too!"

"And your point is?"

"No point. Just sharing important information with you," I laughed.

"Mmm hmm. Thanks. Your father wants to know if you still plan on graduating next month."

"Naturally. I've come too far to stop now. I just wish y'all could make it down here."

"Tina, honey, you know we want to be there. But it's your sister's prom weekend and ..."

"You don't have to explain anything to me. I know and I understand. Besides, I'll be home right after graduation. I have a residency interview up that way.

I still need to decide if I'm going to do my residency down here or up there."

"Just give it to the Lord, Tina. He'll handle everything."

"I know. Look I'm gonna get off this phone. Tell Kim and Daddy hi. Tell Ryan, too, if you talk to him. I'll see you in a few weeks. Love you!"

"Love you too, sugar."

I hung up the phone and leaned against the wall thankful I was in Hot-lanta and not in the snowy, cold-ass city I called home. You'd think deciding where to do my residency would not be such an issue. Hot weather. Cold weather. Occasional snow flurries. Blizzards. Atlanta should win hands down! But the thought of getting on at the world-renowned City Clinic was awesome. The Clinic was top notch.

Whichever locale I chose, assuming the Clinic offered me something, I didn't plan on starting my residency till August. I needed a couple months to just chill out and look at how far I had come. I'd probably spend the month of May, after graduation, at home with my family. I'd stay till my sister's graduation in June. Then, I'd come back down here and either pack or relax.

Life after Mia was uneventful. I hit the books and I hit them hard. I exercised like a demon. I went out with Nicole and Miguel occasionally, but they were just as devoted to their books as I was to mine. I didn't date at all.

After the conversation with my mom, I decided I needed a night out. I hadn't been out since Mia and I broke up. My body was craving attention and the only place I knew where to find a suitor was at the club Mia had taken me to.

Dressed to impress and femmed up to the max, I drove myself to the dark, music thumpin' club. It was a warm night so the place was packed. I immediately went to the bar and ordered two shots of Patron. I needed an instant buzz to calm my nerves. This was the first time I had ever ventured into a club solo.

Shots thrown back and a lemon to chase 'em, I felt a warm sensation take over me. She spoke to me before I saw her.

"Hello, sexy. Long time no see," Mia whispered in my ear.

I turned to face her. "Mia. How have you been?"

"Complaining doesn't get you anywhere, so I'll say I'm doing fine. My mom asked about you."

"Did you tell her we broke up?"

"Nope. I couldn't figure out how to tell them that we are no longer an item."

"How about just telling them the truth?"

"Why tell them the truth when, inside, I'm hoping that we can work through this madness?"

"You've got to be kidding me! Have you turned all your ex-partners loose?" I probed.

"Yes."

I wanted to believe her, but I knew I shouldn't. Just then the dj changed up the music and put on a mellow, slow jam.

"Let's dance," she said as she reached for my hand.

I was just about to say okay when a yellow-boned playa came between us and said to Mia, "Come on, baby. This is my jam."

Mia looked at me and I shook my head knowing that she would never change. When the song was over, she came back to me. "Before you say anything, please believe that I do not know that girl."

"I believe you. I know you aren't interested in studs. But if you were still feeling me, you would have told her no when she asked you to dance."

Mia looked up at the ceiling before she spoke, "When is your jealousy gonna stop?"

"When will you be faithful to me?" I retaliated.

"I was faithful to you!"

"In the physical, maybe. But I need a woman who can love my mind, body, and soul with no distractions!"

"We didn't have any damn distractions!"

"Maybe you didn't. But I was distracted as hell by all your damn exes!"

"I told you you had nothing to worry about!"

"Easy for you to say, I'm sure."

"Tina, you need to toughen the fuck up!" Mia shouted over the music.

"Mia, you need to learn the difference between being in a committed relationship versus dreaming about a committed relationship! And while you're at it, stop telling so many lies!"

"Bitch, please. I brought your ass out of the closet! How are you going to sit here and tell me what I need to stop doing?"

"Mia, you had a hand in helping me confront what I thought were demons. And I thank you for that. But my idea of a committed relationship didn't disappear just because you came into the picture. I know what I want and need. And you, baby girl, aren't it."

"Fuck you, Tina."

"You did. Several times."

"This is exactly why two femmes aren't supposed to be together," Mia shouted. "This is far too much drama for anyone to bear."

"What does being a femme have to do with it?" I asked, annoyed.

"'Cause a stud would've slapped your ass by now."

"Is that right? How do you know your ass wouldn't have been the one to get slapped? You, after all, were the one receiving messages and shit from someone other than me!"

Mia didn't say anything. Then she started laughing. Not like she was insane. She just laughed. "I love you, Tina. Do you know that?"

"Yes, I know you love me. But you were never in love with me. You've yet to fall truly in love."

Mia didn't respond to my observation. Instead she said, "I'm moving to L.A."

"What?"

"Graduation is a month away. I'm packing my bags and heading west. It's time for me to pursue my dreams."

"Mia, that's great. Los Angeles is the city of dreams. I know you're going to do amazing things out there. Maybe you'll even fall in love."

"Maybe."

* * * *

Graduation day came and went. It really wasn't a big deal for me – not like undergrad. All I wanted was to get home to see my family. When I pulled up to the house, after a ten-hour drive, I was tired as hell. When my sister opened the front door and ran to my car to greet me, my energy bounded back with the quickness. Kim had grown into a beautiful young woman since I had last seen her.

"Kim? Oh my goodness! Look at you! You're beautiful!" I hugged her.

"I look just like my big sis."

"Yes you do!" I grinned.

"Both of my girls are beautiful," Mama said as she approached me to give me a hug and welcome me home. "Though I swear I don't know where those crazy green eyes came from. Ryan and your daddy are going to have to beat the men off you with sticks."

"Daddy already is," Kim pouted. I just laughed.

"Mama, did you cook dinner?"

"You know I did! Greens, potato salad, macaroni and cheese, and fried chicken await you in the kitchen, my two-time college graduate!"

"Now that's what I'm talking about. Let's eat!" I linked my arms through theirs and headed towards the front door. My brother Ryan popped up from college for the day. He claimed he made the two-hour drive to see me, but the many loads of dirty clothes in the backseat of his car plus the opportunity to eat mama's fried chicken suggested otherwise.

Ryan, Kim, and I stayed up into the wee hours of Monday morning washing Ryan's clothes and kickin' it like we used to do when we were kids. I don't know what time we fell asleep, but when the clock struck seven, none of us wanted to get up; Kim had to get ready for school, Ryan had to drive back to school, and I had my interview to get ready for.

SHE *Slipped* AND FELL

I always hated the layout of City Clinic because there were so many buildings that comprised the entire facility. The place was like a college campus and in the past, I always managed to go to the wrong building. But this morning luck was on my side because I found the pediatric building with ten minutes to spare. Thankfully, the head of pediatrics invited me into her office right away and the interview took off without a glitch. First, Dr. Lawson talked to me about me. What were my long-term goals? Why the interest in City Clinic? Standard questions. Then she gave me a tour of the facility. Last, she gave me some scrubs and invited me to make a few rounds with her. Making the rounds. I love that part. Interacting with the children is what makes medical school real for me.

The last young patient we visited on this particular morning was a fifteen-month-old girl named Tiara. She was the cutest little thing I had seen all day. Chubby and caramel with jet black hair. Apparently Tiara's little body had been battling pneumonia for the past two weeks. She was having a hard time overcoming the liquid that had settled in her lungs. Tubes seemed to be attached to every inch of her. She looked helpless.

"Where are her parents?" I asked Dr. Lawson. I couldn't imagine not being by her bedside if she were my daughter.

"The mother is usually here around the clock. I haven't seen a father."

At that moment, the door opened to Tiara's hospital room and in walked a frail-looking woman with her head bent over a cup of coffee. When she looked up, I lost my sense of balance as I realized the woman was none other than Kendall.

"Miss Long, it's good to see you this morning. I want to introduce you to a residency candidate. This is Tina Jones."

Kendall's head jerked up as Dr. Lawson spoke my name. Her hand shot up and covered a portion of the left side of her face where her jawbone appeared to be slightly protruding. Her right hand shook vehemently; the coffee splashed onto the floor. Kendall walked towards me. Slowly. I felt tears rising in my eyes as I realized something had gone terribly awry in Kendall's life. I took the cup of coffee from Kendall and set it on the window ledge. I opened my arms and without hesitation, she walked into my hug. Kendall rested her head on my shoulder and I stroked her hair.

Dr. Lawson cleared her throat.

"Dr. Lawson, Miss Long was my roommate when we were in undergrad. She used to be one of my very best friends. I haven't seen or spoken to her in a very long time." Dr. Lawson nodded and left the room.

Kendall retreated from our embrace and held both of my hands. "I can't believe that it's really you," she sniffed.

"Kendall? Kendall, what happened to you?" I asked as my right hand gently brushed her left cheek.

"Oh … My life was forever changed a few years ago. Murder. Rape. This beautiful baby," she said as she went to Tiara's bedside where the girl slept and struggled to take a complete breath.

SHE *Slipped* AND FELL

I walked up beside Kendall and stared down at the pretty little girl realizing she was the splitting image of her mother. I wondered if her eyes were brown with gold flecks as I remembered Kendall's to be. I wrapped my arm around Kendall's shoulders as we stood there and looked down at her tiny little angel.

Reunion

TINA

Though we didn't talk, I stayed with Kendall in Tiara's room for over an hour before I remembered I was at the hospital on business. I promised Kendall I'd be back and then excused myself to go find Dr. Lawson. When I found her, she was very understanding.

"Dr. Lawson, I am so sorry. I haven't seen Kendall in years. I …"

"It's quite alright."

"It's just that she has changed since I last saw her. Her face. The baby. She's so frail," I went on.

"I haven't had the opportunity to get to know Miss Long very well while Tiara's been here, but I sense her heart is troubled and something has been stripped from her. Please, go rebuild your friendship. I think Miss Long needs you. I'll be in touch with you regarding your residency in a few weeks."

"Thank you." Though it was unprofessional, I hugged Dr. Lawson with appreciation for understanding the situation with Kendall. Then, I hurriedly stripped off the hospital scrubs so I could make my way back to Kendall.

As I walked to Tiara's room, memories of Kendall flooded my mind. Friends. Lovers. I missed her. Seeing her today confirmed everything I had felt when I was in Atlanta. I still loved her. And I needed to know what had happened to my friend.

I quietly opened the door to Tiara's hospital room. As I stepped in, I witnessed a mother's love as I watched Kendall hold Tiara tightly in her arms and rock the sleeping child. Kendall stared down at the infant as if Tiara was all that mattered in her life. For reasons I can't explain, tears escaped from the very inner core of my soul and again I wondered what had happened to my friend.

Recovery
KENDALL

When I left the rehabilitation hospital, I left with a reconstructed left jawbone, months of physical therapy for my left arm, in-depth counseling sessions to discuss the loss of my parents and the rape, and I also left with a beautiful baby girl. I named her Tiara because she was my princess and her name started with a "T," like Tina.

When I left the hospital, I had no place to go. No home to speak of. No parents. No friends. I was fortunate that Detective Radcliff kept in close contact with me during my stay at the hospital. He was hopeful I would remember something about the killer. He found Tiara and me a small apartment to hold us over until I felt willing and able to go out and find a place more to my liking. I couldn't go back to my old home – it held too many memories. He also bought us some used furniture and a few clothing items. He said it was the least he could do under the circumstances.

Tiara and I have lived in the apartment ever since. We didn't go out much unless it was to the store or to a doctor's appointment. We got by because my parents had left me a substantial amount of money via their life insurance policies.

Detective Radcliff had made the arrangements for my parents' burial while I was in the hospital. To this day, I have yet to visit their gravesites.

At first, some of my parents' friends would call the apartment and tell me how sorry they were or how bad they felt and how they wished there was something they could do. They'd ask to come over, but I didn't want their sympathy. I just wanted to be left alone and push all thoughts of what had happened out of my head.

The problem, though, was I couldn't make the images go away. In the same instant that I'd visualize my dad's smiling face, I'd see his mutilated body. In the same memory that I'd recall my mama standing in front of the stove in her church clothes, I'd see her lying on my bed with her skirt pushed up above her waist. I couldn't eat. I couldn't sleep. I felt like I was dying, but I knew I had to stay alive for Tiara's sake.

The counselor I was seeing to discuss all the trauma in my life gave me various prescriptions – sedatives, tranquilizers, depression drugs, anxiety drugs. I had a medicine cabinet full of pills, but all the bottles were unopened.

I knew I needed someone to talk to besides the counselor whose only therapy seemed to be pills. I knew I needed a friend. But I didn't have one to call. Sometimes I'd just hold Tiara and talk to her, but then I'd end up feeling guilty because she was far too young for me to be placing so many burdens on.

When I walked into Tiara's hospital room on that May Monday morning, my prayers had been answered, for the second time, in the form of an angel named Tina. Words cannot express how happy and even relieved I was to see her. I knew she was taken aback by my appearance. I didn't look like the young, vibrant college girl she knew and once loved. I knew I had aged. It was in my eyes, my lack of weight, my attitude.

Walking into her coveted embrace was like the beginning of a much needed healing. Seeing Tina again instantly gave me hope and the ability to exhale. And, God, she was so beautiful! Her time in Atlanta had treated her well.

Tina stayed by my side the entire time Tiara was in the hospital. She only left to go to her parent's house to change clothes. During our time together by Tiara's bedside, we had the opportunity to catch up. Tina told me about her friends Nicole and Miguel; about running into Tonio and never returning his calls. I told her about the routine I had settled into after we had graduated; coming home to find my parents' bodies; the rape that I don't remember; waking up in the hospital; the decision behind keeping the baby; and the birth of Tiara.

Through all our conversations, Tina never once mentioned that she was in a relationship.

"Tina, are you dating anyone?"

"I'm flying solo right now."

"There isn't anyone in your life right now?" My eyebrows arched as I asked this question.

She shook her head no as she said, "There was a guy, Lazarus. And a girl, Mia."

"A guy and a girl?"

"I've gone through a self-discovery process while I've been in Atlanta. I've discovered that being with men can be enjoyable – in the friendship sense. But being with women is far better – be it friends or lovers. While I can recognize a nice looking brotha, I'm far more attracted to a beautiful sister. The thought of a penis does not excite me. The thought of a breast, or two," she smiled, "coupled with the softness of a woman, is much more appealing.

"I've finally opened the closed door in my head and let my true self come out. No more pretending to be something I'm not. I've finally accepted who I am and what I like."

"Hmm. Have you told your family?"

"Yes and no," I replied, recalling the telephone conversation with my mom. "I planned on telling them during this trip home, but then I ran into you and simply haven't had the chance to tell them yet."

"I'm sorry for delaying you."

"Kendall, please! Why are you apologizing? There's no other place I'd rather be right now. My sexuality isn't going to suddenly up and disappear! I'll talk to my family about it when I'm sure Tiara is doing better."

"You really are a good friend. I'm so sorry we let so much time come between us."

"Would you stop apologizing? Hindsight is twenty-twenty! Just know that going forward, you can count on me. Okay?"

"Okay." Kendall let some time pass as she rubbed Tiara's head as best as she could without getting her hand tangled up in all the tubes that were hooked up to various machines, monitors, and her child. "Can I ask you another question?"

"Yeah."

"Are you in love with the girl? Mia?"

Tina's green eyes met my sunken brown eyes as she said, "There's only one woman I've ever wanted to love."

I tried to process and digest what Tina had just said. Could it be she still loved me? Four years later? With a child?

I didn't have much time to think about what she had confessed because Tiara let out a whimper. I removed the oxygen mask that had covered her small face and she said something that to my ears sounded a whole lot like, "Mama." I scooped my baby up, tubes and all, and held her close. She was back. She was going to be alright.

A Beautiful Sight
TINA

I watched Kendall remove the oxygen mask from Tiara's tiny face and witnessed the love Kendall was capable of giving. It tugged at my heart to watch Kendall and see a genuine smile spread across her face.

Tiara's bright eyes eventually wandered to me. She pointed at me and smiled. I walked towards her and kissed her tiny button nose. As I stared at Tiara's brown eyes, I was finally able to confirm that they had golden flecks throughout. Just like her mother. I also noticed a tiny little mole on the left corner of her mouth that I hadn't noticed before now, probably because the oxygen mask had covered it up. I studied her cheekbones and soft baby skin. But I was drawn back to the beautiful golden brown eyes and I realized that despite the circumstances in which she was created, there was no way a mother couldn't love her.

I gently rubbed Kendall's back, kissed Tiara again, and left so mother and daughter could be alone. As

I drove to my parents' house, I felt a sense of peace. I was so glad Tiara was out of pneumonia's dark corners. During the week I had been home, I noticed a positive change in Kendall. Maybe it was a sense of relief to not have to go through the waiting alone. Maybe she was genuinely glad to see me. Maybe it was a combination of both. If I truly served as some sort of medicine for Kendall's own internal and even external healing, then it was imperative I continue to give her doses of me.

I hadn't had much time to reflect on Kendall's circumstances because I hadn't been alone much since I'd been home. I'd been by Kendall's side as often as I could. Why had things turned out the way they had? How could I help her believe in herself, and others, again? How could I be the friend she so clearly needed?

I had so many thoughts whirring around in my head that the drive to my parents' house went quickly. When I unlocked the door and walked in, everyone was already in bed so I knew it was late. As I headed to my room, I thought to myself how good it felt to be home and in familiar surroundings. Once I reached the bedroom, I didn't bother to undress. Instead, I kicked off my shoes and welcomed the sight of my childhood bed. I was asleep before my head met the pillow.

Mom, Dad ... I Have Something to Tell You
TINA

The next morning, Saturday, I awoke to sunshine, the smell of coffee perculating and bacon frying in the skillet. The days of my childhood sprung forth; I reached over and, sure enough, my sister had found her way to my bed during the middle of the night. I hit her with my pillow.

"Wake up, sleepy head!"

"Go away," Kim barely muttered.

I sat up and bounced on the bed. "I said get up! Rise and shine! It's Saturday morning. Don't sleep the weekend away!"

Kim slowly rolled onto her back. She rubbed her eyes. "You have way too much energy for a Saturday morning. Why don't you go spend some of it on your mother?"

"Because, little sis, I want to give it all to you! Now wake up!"

Kim groaned. Then she said, "How's your friend's baby doing?"

"I think she's going to be okay. She woke up last night and was actually alert. It's like she did a complete one-eighty."

"Good. Mama and I prayed for her."

I gave Kim a hug before I got out of the bed. "Thanks, kiddo." As I headed towards the bedroom door, I felt a whack on the back of my head.

"No, you didn't," I laughed as Kim sped by me and ran out the room. She had hit me with my own pillow!

"I will redeem myself," I shouted after her and smiled as I recalled the pillow fights we had when we were kids.

Down at the breakfast table, I was surprised to see Ryan. "What are you doing home again?"

He smiled a sheepish grin and said, "Nobody washes clothes like Ma."

"Gee, thanks." Mama set a bowl of scrambled eggs on the table.

The family talked about various things over breakfast when finally the question surfaced. "Tina, who are you dating down there in Atlanta?" Daddy asked.

I put down my fork slowly. I knew what I was about to lay on my family was going to cause major grief, but at the same time, I didn't want any secrets between us.

"I'm single right now, Daddy."

"You mean to tell me all those aspiring doctors and lawyers down there and nobody's knocking on your door?"

"Nope."

"Just 'cause she's fine doesn't mean she's easy to get along with," Ryan jeered.

"Actually, my attitude – or lack of one – has nothing to do with it, Ryan."

"Well, what is it?" Daddy asked.

I took a sip of my coffee before I responded. "Well, Daddy, there are a couple reasons I choose to be single right now. First of all, the amount of schoolwork coupled with my part-time job doesn't allow me much time to date. My main priority, up till now, has been to master my classroom performance. And I have. I'm well on my way to being a pediatrician.

"The second reason I have stayed single is a bit more complicated." I paused to take another sip of my coffee. All eyes were on me. I looked directly at my mother and continued, "Mama, Daddy, Ryan, Kim … I'm a lesbian."

Silence. I looked around the table and saw a different reaction from each family member. From Ryan, I saw a smile. I imagined his college loins perking up as he envisioned what it would be like to have two lesbian women in his bed. A typical male reaction. Kim cried. She had looked up to me her entire life. For the first time, I felt as if I had let her down. Mama nodded in understanding. She, after all, had had a similar conversation with me once before. And Daddy. He was a volcano with hot, molten lava seeping from every crevice of his being.

"No child of mine is going to sit in my house and eat my food if they are homosexual!"

"Okay Daddy." I calmly got up from the table.

"Tina, we didn't raise you to like no damn girls! You're beautiful! Why can't you get a man?" he half asked, half shouted.

I turned around and walked back to the table where they all sat, still staring at me. "I can't get a man because I don't want a man. I don't want a man because I don't like men. I don't like men because there is nothing about the male anatomy or attitude that attracts me to them. What I am attracted to, and have been since as long as I can remember, is women, African-American queens with an inner and outer beauty that no male will ever measure up to.

"I could go into detail about the exact specifications my female significant other must have, but I see no point in sharing such information. It's not important right now. What is important is that you know the truth about me. I've hidden these feelings for so long they've been eating me up inside. I need to be free. The only way I can do that is by being honest with you. If my honesty means you will disown me … well … so be it. But let it be known that I don't want that. I love you guys and I'm not trying to tear us apart. I need for y'all to accept me and who I am.

"If my actions are such that require me to stand before God whom I love and worship, I'll do it because I refuse to believe my God will send me to Hell for wanting love from and giving love to a woman." I paused to catch my breath before I carefully spoke my next words. "I am a lesbian. I am a lover of women. After much inner turmoil, I've accepted who I am. The question is, can you still accept me as your daughter?"

"No."

"Yes."

Daddy and Mama spoke at the same time. They stared at each other as if challenging the other to speak again.

"Yeah, girl," Ryan said. "We'll have to sit down and compare likes and dislikes sometime." He smiled as he shoveled some more eggs into his mouth.

Kim didn't say anything. I respected her silence and prayed for her eventual acceptance.

"Your comments or lack thereof are duly noted. I'm going to shower and get back to the hospital to sit with my friend."

"Take your stuff with you 'cause you're not welcome in this house," Daddy barked. Kim ran out the room.

"Dad," Ryan started.

"Hush boy."

"I'm outta here, man. You don't treat your children like this." Ryan backed away from the table. "Thanks for breakfast," he said as he bent to kiss Mama. He gave me a hug and said, "Keep your chin up, Tina. I'll always love you." He left through the back door.

"Tina, you don't have to leave," Mama said.

"It's okay, Mama. I'll call you and give you a number where you can reach me. I'll be here for a couple more weeks because I want to be here for Kim's graduation. After that, I'm going back to Atlanta. All of a sudden, the decision as to where I'm going to complete my residency has become crystal clear." I tried to leave the room with my head held high. I tried to not be mad at my daddy. But how could I not? He had just kicked me out of his house and his life because of my sexual preference.

When I walked into the bedroom to pack my things, Kim was sitting on my bed.

"Tina, do you really like women? You don't like men? What about all the boyfriends you've had?"

"I was trying to be normal, Kim. I can look at a man and say oh, he's cute or nice abs, nice butt. But it doesn't stir anything up inside of me no matter how hard I try to make it. I've never had pleasurable sex with a man."

"Have you had sex with all your boyfriends?"

"Just two, Tonio and Lazarus. But it's not all about sex. It's the aura that a woman emits. It's her eyes, her lips, her hair, her scent, her mannerisms. It's the total female package."

"Do you have a girlfriend?"

"No."

"Have you ever had a girlfriend?"

"Yes."

"Who acted like the man?"

"Neither one of us. We just acted like ourselves."

"But I thought in a lesbian situation one of the girls is a girl and the other is a man."

"Kim, who told you that? Television? The newspaper? What you're talking about is roles. Yeah, some lesbian relationships get caught up in the femme, soft stud, stud or butch titles, but I don't. Honestly, I'm not even attracted to females that look like guys. But that's not to disrespect those who do. All I'm saying is in my relationships, it wasn't about roles. It was about being in love and being strong where the other person is weak and vice versa."

"Okay. So what you're telling me is you like cover-girl women, model types."

"Pretty much."

"And you don't dress like a man or anything so you still act like a regular girl?"

"That's right."

"So it's like a friendship, but you also have sex."

"Umm … I'd say it's a little bit deeper than that. It's a relationship. Just like a man and a woman have a relationship. There's no difference."

"So how many girlfriends have you had?"

"Two."

"Did you um … did y'all …"

"Yes. We made love."

"You loved them? How did y'all do it? "

"Slow down, Kim! First of all, I am not about to sit here and share the intimate details of my sex life with you. All you need to know is sex between two women is possible and enjoyable."

"Have I ever met them?"

"You know one of them very well. Remember Kendall?"

"Kendall? Your best friend Kendall?"

"One and the same."

"If she's gay, why does she have a daughter?"

"I'm not sure she's gay. I think she was just experimenting when we were together. But I still need to clarify that with her. Anyway, she has a daughter because she walked in on the brutal murder of her parents and the perpetrator beat, stabbed, and raped her."

"Dang! That's horrible! Wait a minute. I remember hearing something like that on the news a year or so ago. That was our Kendall? The one that used to be here, like, all the time? Oh my God! They never released her name! I didn't know it was Kendall!"

"Yeah. Her mother and father were killed during that attack. Life sucks sometimes, huh?"

"Yeah. Tina, why didn't you come see her when all this happened?"

"I didn't know."

"But y'all are best friends!"

"We were, but we lost touch."

"And now you've been reunited?"

"Yep."

"What are the odds of that happening?" Kim asked. Before I could answer, she said, "So let me get this straight. You dumped Tonio for Kendall. You and Kendall broke up before you moved to Atlanta. You tried to date a dude again. What was his name? Um … Lazarus. You and Lazarus broke up. Then you dated some other chick, but it didn't work out and you haven't been with anybody else 'cause you really only care for one and that's Kendall? Damn! She must have put it on you!" Kim smiled.

"Yeah. Yeah she did."

"Do you still love her?"

"Yeah."

"Well, go get your girl, Tina!" Kim said as she stood up from the bed and gave me a hug.

"You're okay with this?"

"Hell yeah! Besides, I need a place to stay when I start classes at Unity in August," she said slyly.

"Unity?"

She reached under the mattress of my bed and pulled out a stack of college acceptance letters that she had been hiding. The top letter was from Unity.

"I haven't told Mama and Daddy yet. I was waiting to see where you were going to do your residency. Seeing how things turned out here this morning, I'm guessing you're going back to Atlanta, right?"

"Right," I said hesitantly.

"Well, I'm going with you. I got a full scholarship to Unity. They've been hounding me for the past two months for a decision. I told them that I wouldn't know for sure until after I graduated. Now I know. My mind's made up."

I gave Kim the biggest hug I could possibly give her.

"So does this mean I can stay with you?"

"Hell yeah!" I mocked her from a few minutes earlier.

"Good. Now, Tina?"

"Huh?"

"Go get your girl."

Love For You

TINA

The drive over to the hospital passed by quickly. I don't know if it was because I was speeding or because I spent the entire drive reflecting on the morning events. I was proud of myself for staying calm despite my father's outburst. But most importantly, my soul was free!

As I walked into Tiara's hospital room, Kendall was there posted at her bedside and Tiara was sitting up in the bed playing with a stuffed animal. Tiara looked and pointed at me as I entered the room.

Kendall sounded out my name slowly, "Tee-na."

"Na," Tiara repeated. She was pretty sharp for a fifteen-month-old.

I walked over to Kendall and gave her a hug. I also bent over the bed and kissed Tiara on the cheek.

"Looks like the patient has recovered," I smiled.

"Dr. Lawson said she's doing much, much better. There's still some fluid in her lungs. Maybe another week in here, then I can take her home."

"That's wonderful news!"

"Tell me about it." Kendall tilted her head to the side before she said, "Why are you glowing?"

I smiled and answered, "I'm free, Kendall. I told my entire family this morning over breakfast. I'm finally free ... to be ... just me."

"Whoa! What did they say?"

"Dad's pissed. He kicked me out of the house."

"Oh my God!"

"It's okay. I'm not trippin'. I'll get a hotel room for the next two weeks or stay with a cousin. After Kim's graduation, I'm going back to Atlanta to start my residency."

"You're not staying?"

"I can't. It's all good, though. Kim's going to go back with me. She got a full scholarship to Unity."

"Wow. That's great," Kendall's voice was flat.

"Kendall? What's wrong?"

"Nothing. I've just gotten used to you being here. I'm going to miss you."

"Come with me."

"I can't come with you."

"Why not?"

"I ... My parents ... My job ... Tiara," she said unconvincingly.

"Your parents are gone. You can get a job in Atlanta. Tiara is too young to care."

"I ..."

"Let me be your family."

"I don't want your pity, Tina. This isn't high school. You don't have to rescue me."

"I know this isn't high school. I don't have any pity to give you. What I do have ... what I've always had ... is love for you."

"You don't love me. How could you possibly still love me? I hurt you. Remember? And look at me! Look at my face!"

"I never stopped loving you, Kendall. Don't make your decision today. Just think about it," I said as I reached to pick up Tiara.

Later that evening Kendall did two things that really touched my heart. First, she asked me to be Tiara's godmother. And second, she asked me to stay at her apartment. I agreed to both.

Uncertain

KENDALL

I wasn't sure that I would take Tina up on her offer to move to Atlanta. While she was correct in that there was no reason for me to stay here, I found it hard to believe she could still love me after the way I'd treated her so many years ago. And I was extremely self-conscious about the scar on my left jawbone from the reconstructive surgery. I no longer felt beautiful. I only felt violated. In fact, Tina deserved someone better than me.

But while she was in town, I wanted to spend as much time with her as possible. Asking her to be Tiara's godmother was natural. There was no one more deserving or fitting than Tina. She'd be a good godmother and I sincerely hoped that she and Tiara could develop a special relationship.

Asking her to stay at my place also seemed natural. I wouldn't be using the apartment anyway. As long as Tiara was in the hospital, that's where I'd be. Tina, on the other hand, needed someplace to lay her head at night. It wasn't necessary that she spend her entire vacation sitting at the hospital with me! I offered her my apartment because that's what friends do.

I always knew Tina would come out one day. Well, not always, but definitely after our relationship. When she was willing to be open about our relationship back in college I figured it was only a matter of time before she'd be true to herself. I was proud of her. At least she knew who she was. And she didn't give a damn what other people thought. Good for her. I wished I could be half as strong.

Give Me Strength
TINA

Some things never change. When I walked into Kendall's apartment, all I could do was shake my head and laugh. It was a mess! Clothes on the floor. Food on the counter. The television was on. I immediately began to clean and straighten up. I dusted, stripped the bed and crib, put clean linens and towels out. I even went grocery shopping for her.

Kendall's apartment didn't have much character to it. There weren't any special touches or pictures hanging on the walls. No photo albums. No knick-knacks. Just the basics. Couch, chair, table, television, kitchen table, bed, crib. It was almost as if Kendall had purposely avoided making this house her home, maybe because she had always considered her parents' house her home. Was it possible that the murders and the rape had affected her even more than I initially imagined?

Dr. Lawson said Kendall could bring Tiara home at the end of the week. So, when I wasn't at the hospital with Kendall, I spent my time making sure

Tiara's homecoming was a warm one. I bought stuffed animals and toys, a new blanket for her crib, and flowers for the weary mommy. I drove Kendall and Tiara home from the hospital. When Kendall opened the door to her apartment and stepped inside, a huge smile spread across her face.

"You cleaned it! You weren't s'pose to clean my place!"

"How else could I stay here? This place was a pigsty."

"I'll admit there were a few dirty dishes, but other than that, it was fine," Kendall said guiltily.

"Fine my ass."

Kendall laughed. "Look, Tiara. No dust!"

Tiara grinned, but she was far more interested in the bright red roses I had placed on the living room table.

"You bought me flowers?"

"You deserve 'em mommy,"

"Thank you," Kendall said as she hugged me.

As I held her in my arms, I let my hands drop to her waist. Then I pulled back and stared deeply into her eyes.

"I've missed you, Kendall."

"I missed you too," she said as her hand rubbed the back of my neck. I mistook the rub as an invitation. I bent my head towards her for a long-awaited kiss, but Kendall turned away.

"I'm sorry."

"No, don't be sorry. You know, Tina, I haven't been intimate with anyone since you. But someone was intimate with me without my permission. I'm still trying to work through that."

"I understand," I said as I kicked myself for trying to kiss her. How callous of me to do that! But I still held her close. Why did being with her always feel so right?

Kendall finally removed herself from my clutches and wandered into the kitchen. "What's that delicious smell?"

"Ramen Noodles," I replied teasingly, referring to our college days. Kendall laughed. "Just playing. There's a pot roast in the oven. Fresh green beans. Mashed potatoes with gravy made especially for the little lady. And a fresh pineapple just for you."

"Damn! Can I keep you?"

"Only if you come with me to Atlanta." Why was Kendall waiting so long to confirm with me that she'd make the trip?

"Well, we need to feed the little lady pretty quickly or else she's going to be asleep for the night."

I looked over at Tiara who was half playing, half sleeping on her new stuffed teddy bear. I needed a camera because this was definitely a Kodak moment.

"Right. You get the baby. I'll fix our plates."

Dinner was quiet, but comfortable. Sure enough, Tiara went to sleep after her meal of mashed potatoes, which, by the way, she loved.

Kendall helped me clean up the dishes and kitchen, which was a first. She never cleaned the kitchen when we lived together in college. Then we took showers and got our pajamas on. Kendall was already in her bed when I got out of the shower. I grabbed a pillow and blanket out of her linen closet and got comfortable on the couch. I had just turned the television on and lowered the volume when I felt a familiar stare. I looked up and Kendall, clad in hot pink shorts and a white t-shirt that hugged the hell out of her breasts, walked towards me. Without a word she took the remote from my hand and turned the television off. I instinctively knew not to protest. She held her hand out and waited for me to take it. So I did. She gently pulled me up off the couch and led me to her bedroom. She lay down first. I lay down beside her.

"I just want to sleep and not have nightmares. I want to close my eyes and not see images that I can't erase. I've always felt safe in your arms. Please, just hold me tight tonight, Tina."

"I'm here." I intertwined my legs with hers and held her close to me.

A Mother's Love

TINA

This was the first time I had seen my daddy since he had kicked me out of the house when I revealed to the family that I am a lesbian. We didn't say more than two words to each other. His hi plus my hi equaled the two words. Regardless of our lack of communication, my mama made it clear that this was Kim's day and under no circumstances was it to be ruined.

"Whatever differences y'all have need to be pushed under the table," Mama said as we sat in the bleachers before the ceremony started. "Kim's the star today. Our baby girl is graduating, with honors, got a full scholarship to a good school, and leaves in less than a week to start a new chapter in her life. So, Tina, you and your father need to squash the petty bullshit."

Ryan and I looked at each other in disbelief. Did our down-home, church-going mama just say bullshit? Ryan busted out laughing.

"Daaannnggg! Mama, next time emphasize the 'ull'."

"Shut up, boy!" Mama replied. Even Daddy smiled.

The ceremony started and in walked my baby sister decked out in her cap, gown, and various ropes signifying her participation in numerous school clubs. Kim was the class valedictorian and it seemed that she received every honor a high school graduate could receive. Her classmates cheered her on every time she was called up to the podium. I was so proud of her.

After the ceremony, Kim found us in the crowded gymnasium and gave out hugs. After pictures, Kim announced she was going out with her friends and left us standing there.

"I don't know why y'all are standing there with puppy dog eyes," Mama said to Ryan and me. "Both of you did the same thing when you graduated from high school. Kiss, kiss, hug, hug, bye."

"Ma, I never would have left y'all hanging like that," from Ryan. "I would have asked Pop for some money before I said 'bye'!"

"Boy!" Mama laughed.

"Well, I'm off," I said. "I'm going to see if I can persuade Kendall into going to dinner and a movie with me. She needs to get out of that apartment."

"Who's going to watch the baby?" Mama asked.

"Um ... nobody. If she says yes, we'll just take Tiara with us."

"If she says yes, just bring the baby to the house. Your mama and I will keep her. That baby needs to see somebody 'sides her mother," Daddy said.

Once again Ryan and I looked at each other in disbelief. First Mama cusses and now Daddy is offering to babysit so his lesbian daughter can go out on a semi-date. Daammmnnn!

"Plus, we haven't had a baby in the house in quite some time," Mama said. Then as an afterthought, "And, Ryan, that does *not* mean we want *you* to bring any babies home, either!"

"Hey, between the two of us," Ryan said pointing at me and himself, "I'm your best bet for providing you with grandchildren!" Even Daddy laughed at that as I swung at my brother and connected with his jaw.

I unlocked the door to Kendall's apartment and walked in where I discovered both mommy and baby sleeping peacefully on the couch. I closed the door gently so not to disturb them and headed to Kendall's room to change my clothes. When I passed by the couch I paused only for a second and watched them sleep. Kendall's breaths were long and quiet. Tiara's were short and fuzzy. Tiara kept smiling in her sleep. My great-grandmother once told me that when a baby smiles in her sleep it means she's playing or dancing with angels. Tiara was a beautiful little angel herself. I wondered what the other angels looked like. I wondered if Mr. and Mrs. Long were among the angels that she was playing with.

Then my eyes drifted to Kendall. She had put on some weight since the first day I saw her at the hospital. Her face wasn't sunken in anymore. Her hair had gotten back some of its vibrancy. Despite the scar on her left cheek, she still resembled the girl I fell in love with just a few short years ago.

Suddenly Kendall's eyebrows drew in tightly and her breaths became quick and haggard. Her mouth twitched and I could see her pulse racing in her neck. Then, just as quickly as it started, it stopped. Nightmare. I shared the bed with Kendall and held her tight every night; whenever she had a bad dream, her body showed signs such as these. Sometimes she had them two or three times a night. Other times, she'd sleep without disruption.

Holding her soft body next to mine at night and watching her rest like I was doing now always reminded me of the night not so long ago when we were in college and I stood in her doorway and watched her study. The feelings I felt that night – the need to protect, nurture, and love her forever – always re-surfaced.

Just then, Kendall's eyes fluttered open and she blinked a few times until her eyes adjusted to the semi-darkness.

"Tina?"

"Hey sweetie. You okay?"

"Mmm hmm. Fine," she paused. "Why are you staring at me like that?"

"Like what?"

"Like you have something very heavy on your mind."

"I don't know. Maybe I do. Hey, what do you say to going out to dinner and catching a movie?"

"I don't think Tiara will sit through a movie. Especially since she's napping right now. She'll be wide awake and talking through the whole thing."

"My parents said they'd keep her."

"Your parents?"

"Yeah. Can you believe that? Actually, it was my dad's idea. Once he voiced it, my mama was all over it. They love babies and there hasn't been any over to the house in a long time."

"Oh. Well ... okay, I guess."

"Good! Let me change my clothes then I'll call Mama and let her know we're on our way."

The ride to my parent's house was quiet. I think Kendall was trying to convince herself she could leave Tiara for a few hours and not go crazy from separation. I was quiet because I was trying to think of reasons why Kendall should come back to Atlanta with me and Kim.

When we got to my parent's house, Daddy was waiting at the door. When we got to the door, Mama took Tiara from Kendall and an instant bond was developed. Tiara looked at both of my parents, gave my mama a hug, and pooted. Daddy laughed and then Tiara laughed and it was at that moment Kendall broke down and cried.

Mama handed the baby to Daddy and shooed them away to the tv room. Mama took Kendall by the hand and led her to the kitchen. I followed behind them.

"Sugar, it's okay," Mama said as she pulled Kendall into a hug and stroked her hair.

"I'm ... I'm ... so sorry. I haven't seen you all in so long. My parents ... They would have given anything to have a grandbaby. Seeing you with Tiara ... it just ... it just ..." Kendall cried.

"Shhh. Baby, it's okay. Your parents are resting with the Lord now. Shhh," Mama continued to hold Kendall and stroke her hair.

I leaned against the wall and took it all in. Why hadn't I realized what Kendall needed more than anything all this time was a mother's love and touch? If anybody could heal Kendall, my mama could. So I slipped out of the room quietly and joined my daddy and Tiara in the tv room where I discovered that my daddy had already taught Tiara how to make farting noises with her mouth.

Finding Me
KENDALL

When Tiara smiled at Mr. and Mrs. Jones the tears surfaced like a raging white squall that had been swirling around and around in my body, but unable, up until now, to find the right outlet. Walking into Mrs. Jones' arms was like walking into the arms of my mother. Oh how I missed her.

I never got to kiss my parents goodbye. When I saw them the morning of the attack, Mama was at the stove frying bacon and Daddy was sitting at the kitchen table reading the paper and drinking a cup of coffee. I assumed when I left the house that morning, late for work, I'd kiss them when I got home later that evening. I assumed their day would be happy, restful, and uneventful. I assumed Mama would have some sort of monstrous meal prepared by the time I got home from work. I assumed ... I assumed ... I assumed ...

As Mrs. Jones stroked my hair the emptiness I had been living with since their death finally began to fill. A mother's love was bestowed upon me and though she was not my mother, her love was as close to it as I had received in a very, very long time.

Tina and I didn't go out that night after all. Mrs. Jones kept me in the kitchen most of the evening and fed my soul as only a mother can. Once she was satisfied that I was full, only then did she allow me to leave the kitchen and go into the tv room with Tiara, Tina, and Mr. Jones.

We spent the remainder of the evening playing Scrabble and eating pizza. Tiara had a permanent spot on Mr. Jones' lap. She was entranced by his loud, booming voice and infectious laugh. And she loved the way his beard felt when she rubbed her hand against it.

Tina's parents took Tiara and me in that night and welcomed us as their own. When we had completed the game (Tina won by spelling a medical term that wasn't even in the common folks' dictionary) and Tina's dad sat in his chair, her mom sat in her rocker and rocked Tiara to sleep, and Tina and I sat on the couch barely touching (as I could never disrespect her folks in that manner especially since Tina's lesbian announcement was so new), I knew I had a family and a home again.

I was emotionally drained as Tina and I drove back to my apartment. Even so, I couldn't wait to lay Tiara in her crib and talk to Tina.

Tina headed straight for the shower. I changed Tiara out of her clothes, into her pajamas, and put her to sleep in her crib. I searched the apartment for a candle, some matches, and a slow-jam CD. The shower cut off just as I hit the play button on the CD and lit the candle.

Tina walked into my bedroom and stopped in her tracks. I was sitting on the edge of my bed.

"You okay?" she asked hesitantly. I could smell the flower-scented shower gel she used while taking her shower.

"I'm fine."

"Okay," she said, still unsure of my mood.

She bent over her suitcase and folded up the pants she had worn. I walked up behind her and placed my hands on her waist. She froze, not sure what I was seeking. Truth be told, I wasn't sure what I wanted either, but I figured together we would find out.

Tina turned and faced me. Her green eyes searched mine. Her eyes always seemed to penetrate deep into my soul. I opened up and let her peek inside. I raised both my hands and held her face as I spoke, "I love you, Tina. Let me love you right this time." I slowly nibbled on her bottom lip.

Tina's arms went around my waist and our tongues rediscovered what was once very familiar. Tina was gentle with me and only went places that I encouraged her to go.

My Temple
TINA

When she held my face and said, "I love you, Tina," I didn't hear the rest. I felt her soft lips descend upon my own and welcomed her to me like I never had before.

Even though Kendall initiated the lovemaking, I did all the loving that night. I wanted to show her that while her body had indeed been violated, it truly was a temple and I was ready, willing, and able to worship it.

We took it slow. Tender kisses and sensual caresses. I was surprised at Kendall's responsiveness to me. It was as if she had been craving my every touch. And though we hadn't been intimate with one another in several years, rediscovering what was once well known, was like tasting my favorite flavor of ice cream. Sugary and sweet. And if I dripped or missed a spot, I was quick to lick it up and savor the flavor for as long as I could before it traveled down my core.

Our lovemaking and reunion lasted for hours. The scent of her was on my fingers, my tongue, my breath. I traced the scars on her chest, where she had been stabbed, with my lips. I whispered testimonies of her everlasting beauty and strength. Finally, when we were both spent and I was satisfied that some of the negative memories of her last sexual experience had been partially, but not completely removed as I knew that would take some time, and I received confirmation from Kendall that our lovemaking was pleasurable to her and not harmful or intrusive, we lay in each others arms and I was able to reflect on all that had just happened.

"I love you. Come to Atlanta with me."

Kendall did not hesitate. "When do we leave?"

Packin'

KENDALL

Packing up my apartment was a piece of cake. There wasn't much to pack. I never made this place my home. Venturing to my parents' home was a different matter. Even though the house had been empty for a while, a lot of my things, their things, were still inside. Tina and her parents went with me to gather the items.

Entering my home was difficult. I stepped over the spot where my dad died. I could still envision him there. I didn't want to step on the memory. I walked deeper into the kitchen. I could see Mama at the stove cooking up something spectacular. Daddy was sitting at the kitchen table reading his newspaper and drinking a cup of coffee. The lump in my throat was thick as I remembered these things.

Through the kitchen and into the living room. I ran my finger across the coffee table and picked up one of our many family pictures. The tears came far too quickly as I recalled their laughter.

Up the stairs to my room. A momentary pause outside the door. Mama was killed in my room. I was raped in my room. I took a long, deep breath and pushed open the door. It creaked. My bed was gone. The forensic people must have removed it. It didn't matter. I could still see her on my bed. I could smell the blood. My heartbeat increased. Tina's hand stroked my hair. I jumped. I hadn't heard her come up behind me. I turned to her as my body convulsed and the tears flowed. She didn't say anything. She just stroked my hair and held me tight.

We didn't stay in the house long. I couldn't. Mr. and Mrs. Jones packed the things they thought I would want. As they loaded the stuff into the car, I closed the door and left the key in the mailbox. I didn't look back.

A Fresh Start

TINA

No one said the move to Atlanta was going to be easy. We had to rent a U-Haul for Kim's stuff plus clothes and a few household items from Kendall's place. We decided we didn't need Kendall's furniture since I already had some. Ryan bought Kendall's furniture from her because he was going to move off-campus for the upcoming school year.

We hitched Kim's car to the back of the U-Haul. Ryan offered to help us drive down to Atlanta as long as I bought him a plane ticket to get back home. I agreed. So Ryan and Kim drove the U-Haul and Kendall, Tiara, and I rode in my car. When it was all said and done, the trip took about fifteem hours because the U-Haul couldn't go much faster than fifty-five. Kendall's car was left behind. We'd have to make a separate trip, later in the year, to bring it down.

By the time we reached my small, one-bedroom apartment, Tiara was crabby, Ryan and Kim were arguing over something trivial, Kendall was tired from dealing with Tiara, and I was cranky because there was no way in hell we'd all sleep comfortably in my small apartment. Yet when we walked into my place, everyone was so glad to be able to stand and stretch, the size of my apartment wasn't as daunting as I initially thought it would be. First task for tomorrow was to check with the landlord and see if any three-bedrooms were available.

As luck would have it, I was able to sign a lease for a three-bedroom apartment the next morning. My landlord wanted us to wait a few weeks before we moved in so he could have the carpet cleaned and add some fresh paint. I explained to him that time was of the essence and we'd take the apartment as is. I needed to utilize Ryan's strength while he was in town. Whatever cleaning or painting that needed to be done could be handled by us girls. I called Miguel to have him lift some of the heavier stuff with Ryan. By six o'clock that evening our new apartment was clean from top to bottom. The carpet had been cleaned with those carpet cleaners you rent from the hardware store, Tiara's room was painted pink, the furniture had been moved, and all of the clothes and boxes were stacked in the appropriate rooms. The place had yet to be organized, but Kendall, Kim, Tiara, and I had a place that we could now call home.

Ryan stayed with us for two weeks. He slept on the couch and familiarized himself with Atlanta's women, streets, and nightlife. Kim utilized her time by finding a job and walking around Unity's campus.

Kendall surprised me. Instead of applying for work at accounting firms, she looked for a position within the various crisis centers in Atlanta. She no longer wanted to work with numbers. She wanted to be a rape counselor to young women.

"Kendall, when did you decide to make this career change?" I asked her over dinner one night.

"I decided during the trip down here. I'm ready to start my life over, but I can't do that sitting behind a desk crunching numbers, not when I know there are thousands, if not millions, of girls who are going through the same thing I did. I need to help as many victims as I can. I need to let them know there can be sunshine after the storm."

"Yes. There can be," I agreed with her.

"I think I want to work part-time and go back to school part-time. I think I'll take up counseling or psychology or something. I need to check and see which degree would be most applicable to the help I want to offer these girls. And I also want to see if any of the programs down here include drum counseling. When I went through my healing time at home, I was placed in a drum therapy course and I found it to be very effective."

"That's awesome, Kendall," Kim said. "And I can help out with Tiara when I'm not working or in class." She reached over to Tiara and squeezed her cheek. Already Kim and Tiara had developed a sisterly bond. Tiara smiled when Kim tickled her chin.

"We'll all chip in. Surely we can work something out so everyone here benefits. I see no reason to have to put Tiara into daycare. Plus, don't forget, Miguel and Nicole can help, too. They're already in love with Tiara," I said.

"Thank you. I don't know what I'd do without you two," Kendall said.

"No thanks needed. I would, however, like to hear more about the drum therapy you mentioned. When you're ready, I mean. You don't have to tell me right this sec," I said.

"I'll share the entire recovery with you. I promise."

A few days later Kendall got the opportunity she had been waiting for. A woman from a crisis center in Decatur called her for an interview. After Kendall shared her story with the lady, she was hired on the spot. The best part was that Kendall got to choose her own work schedule. Kendall opted to work nights with the understanding that once she started school, she could adjust her schedule accordingly.

So all in all, things started off well for everyone. Everyone got along. Everyone had a job. But even with all the forward movement, Kendall and I weren't officially together as the words had not been outwardly spoken. Yet we shared a room and a bed and many intimate moments. At first I wondered how my sister Kim would react knowing I was sharing my bed with Kendall. But Kim could care less and she told me so one morning before she left for work.

"I heard some interesting noises coming from your room last night, big sister," she said with a knowing smile.

I blushed as I recalled the night of passionate lovemaking Kendall and I shared.

"Don't blush! I didn't mean to embarrass you. Do you know how many times I've heard Mama and Daddy get busy?"

"No. And I'd prefer not to."

"Why do you look so embarrassed?"

"I don't know. This isn't the type of conversation I want to have with my younger sister. Would it be better for you, make you more comfortable, if Kendall slept in Tiara's room?" I asked.

"Who said I was uncomfortable?"

"No one. I just thought … I never asked you how you would feel if Kendall and I slept in the same room. That was very inconsiderate of me. I'm sorry."

"Tina, please! I know how you feel about Kendall. And I think she feels the same way about you. I just want you to be happy. And if Kendall makes you happy, I'm all for it. I don't care where she sleeps," Kim smiled at me. "Furthermore, once I meet me a good man, I might want him to stay with me from time to time," she smiled shyly.

"Oh great. Bribery!"

Kim smiled, grabbed an apple, and headed out the door.

Commitment

TINA

Little did I know just how soon Kim would meet a young male friend. Kim worked at the coffee shop right off campus. It was the same coffee shop where Mia and I had met. Never one to meet a stranger, Kim recognized and got to know the regular customers in a very short time.

One morning Kim was greeted by a deep baritone voice and a smile sexy enough to melt the sugar off a cookie. He stood about six feet tall and had skin the color of a brand new copper penny. He had short twisties in his hair, a chiseled body reminiscent of a gladiator, and a clean-shaven, silky-smooth baby face. His name was Kwame and from the moment he spoke (he said hello and ordered an iced vanilla coffee), Kim was hooked. Once Kim prepared his coffee, handed it to him, smiled, and let the infamous Jones green cat eyes stare directly into his, Kwame never again looked at another woman and instead, became a semi-permanent fixture at our apartment.

Don't get me wrong. I liked Kwame. It was just weird to watch my baby sister fall in love. Her world revolved around him and his world revolved around her. He was a music major and spent quite a bit of time writing Kim songs on the portable keyboard that he always seemed to have within arm's reach. He didn't smoke or cuss. He seemed to be a good guy. He was a local, as he grew up in College Park. The youngest of nine, he was simply trying to make a better life for himself. Hell, I couldn't fault that at all.

Kim was so funny the first time he came to the apartment. She introduced Kwame to Kendall and me. Then, right in front of us, she asked him, "How do you feel about homosexuality?"

Kwame didn't miss a beat. He immediately responded, "While I personally am not homosexual, I don't discriminate against those who are."

"Good," Kim replied, "because Kendall and my sister are lovers. If that makes you uncomfortable or if you feel the need to criticize, you need to step. Tina's my sister, my family. Her feelings matter to me. If you disrespect Tina or Kendall, you disrespect me and I will not be disrespected."

"Duly noted," Kwame replied. Then they smiled at each other and went into the kitchen. Kendall and I stared at each other in disbelief and amusement.

"My sister is a true mess."

"Yes, she is."

"But I love her."

"So do I. And you know Tiara would be lost without her."

"I know."

"So … Tina … is that what we are? Lovers?"

"Well, I am in love with you. And I do make love to you. So, yeah, I guess so."

"It sounds impersonal to me. Kind of casual. How about life partners?" Kendall asked.

I smiled, "Are you sure you're ready?"

"More than you'll ever know."

Something to Consider
TINA

Summer came to a close sooner than anybody wanted it to. But we were all settled into a comfortable routine of work, school, and sleep. Well, everybody that is, except me. Being a resident didn't allow me much time for normalcy. I spent many a night in the doctors' lounge at the hospital just trying to catch a quick nap.

I worked under the direction of a pediatric expert who also happened to be a black woman, Dr. Jeanette Mitchell. Her life was the modern-day success story. She grew up the youngest in a family of ten, poverty-stricken. The father left for work one day and never came back. The mother worked three jobs. A couple of the boys got in trouble. One died by trying to live the fast life. The others worked factory jobs. Most of the girls were pregnant before they completed high school. The others dropped out and married. Jeanette was the only one who went to college. She received a few scholarships, but she primarily footed the bill by working two jobs and sleeping only when depravity was no longer an option. She ate even less than she slept and once mentioned that a peanut butter and jelly sandwich was a delicacy where she came from. She graduated at the top of her class in undergrad and medical school. She landed the prestigious Director of Pediatric Care position after four years of dedicated hard work and long hours.

The sister was in her mid-forties and she sported a short, freeze-curl hairstyle with auburn tints. She had a mahogany complexion, stood five feet seven inches easy, and couldn't possibly weigh more than a buck fifty. When she spoke, it was with clarity and diction. When she walked, it was with purpose and poise. Though she never flaunted her earned wealth, it was visible via her car, a top-of-the-line, two-door convertible Mercedes; her clothes, designer; and her gold – and diamond – jeweled presence.

When I learned she would be my mentor, I was intimidated because the sister's name is known in Atlanta. She served on various community and corporate boards in the city. She was a frequent keynote speaker at galas and five hundred dollar-a-plate fundraising dinners. The *Atlanta-Journal and Constitution* often quoted her on issues that dealt with child well-being.

My apprehension was put to rest during our first meeting.

"Tina Jones, it's a pleasure to meet you." Dr. Mitchell walked towards me with an outstretched hand.

"Likewise. It's a pleasure to work under your directorship, Dr. Mitchell," I replied as I shook her hand.

"Well, if I'm going to be your mentor, please call me Jeanette. Save Dr. Mitchell for the hospital floor."

"Okay Dr. Mitch … I mean Jeanette."

Jeanette showed me a relaxed smile before she continued. "Tell me about yourself."

"Well, I got my undergrad from …"

"No, sweetie. I read about your academic background on your application and transcript. I'm more interested in hearing about your professional aspirations. Tell me what drives you and what frustrates you. What are your sources of support right now as this will be the most challenging time of your entire medical career to date? Where do you see yourself ten years down the road?" Jeanette probed.

"I see. Well. My motivation stems from my desire to succeed at whatever I do. I don't know failure. Plus I have a younger brother and sister, both of whom are in college right now, and I have to set the bar for them. I chose medicine because when I was little I would see those save-the-children commercials on tv. They'd film kids who were deprived of food, clothing, and health care and it tore at my heart every time those commercials would come on. The makers of the commercials said a quarter a day would help to feed and clothe those kids. I wanted to do more than that. I wanted to make them all healthy and happy. That feeling never left me as I grew older. So I chose pediatric medicine as my goal.

"What frustrates me? That's a bit more complicated. I think when my life lacks balance, I get easily frustrated and bothered. I look at it like this: my life has three dimensions - home, work, and school. If my home life is out of whack, then work and school may suffer a bit. If I'm stressed from work or school, then my home life will feel it. When things are good in each of those three areas, my life has balance and I function at optimal levels. When one is off kilter, I get frustrated and have to work harder so everything doesn't fall to crap." I paused to reflect on my sudden realization of what frustrated me.

Dr. Mitchell – I mean Jeanette – nodded her head in understanding. "Continue," she said.

"Okay. My sources of support include my family and my girl."

"Your girl?"

"Yes. My girlfriend. I guess I should tell you, Jeanette, I am a lesbian."

"I see," Jeanette said. Then, "How do you think your lifestyle will affect your work in regards to attracting and retaining clients?"

"To be honest, I never thought about it."

"Perhaps you should. I say this because you just admitted to me that you are a lesbian. I'm assuming that you consider yourself 'out.' Does that mean you are going to be forthcoming with this information to your clients?"

I thought about it before I answered her. I think I understood where she was going with her new line of questioning, but I wasn't one hundred percent sure. If I tell my patients or the parents of my patients that I am a lesbian, the whole homophobia issue could present itself. Maybe the parents of my girl clients would not want me to touch their daughters. This, of course, is a ridiculous thought as I am not a child molester or pedophile. I don't desire children by any stretch of the imagination.

"What would you recommend?"

She looked at me intently. "From one sister to another, Tina, I recommend that you do what's comfortable for you. There are no laws that state a homosexual person cannot be a pediatric doctor. Likewise, there are no rules that state that a pediatric doctor must reveal his or her sexual preference to his or her clients. As a matter of fact, by admitting your lifestyle preference, you may increase your chance of lawsuits because there aren't any laws to protect your lifestyle, either. By keeping such information a secret, you have to question the honest and ethical relationship that you are keeping from your patients.

"This is a tough decision to make. I can only recommend, from sister to sister, that you do what's right for you."

Man! This was an issue that I had given absolutely no consideration to prior to now. And why did Jeanette keep saying "from sister to sister?" I mean, I know she's black, hence, my sister. Or was she a sister meaning in the same lifestyle as myself? If she's a lesbian, I never heard about it in the media. Maybe she was on the down-low and was encouraging me to be as well. Whatever she was saying to me, I knew I couldn't make a decision right then and there so I tucked the information away for future internal debate.

"Thank you. I'm going to give this issue a lot of thought before I make a decision."

"I understand. For now, your secret is safe with me."

"But it's not a secret," I said.

"I'll keep it safe anyway."

SHE *Slipped* AND FELL

And that's how our first meeting concluded. I wasn't sure what to make of Jeanette. Was she straight? Was she a lesbian? Was she trying to protect me? I honestly didn't know. Perhaps I'd figure it out as time pressed on.

Sister My Ass

TINA

I spent my birthday on duty at the hospital. The staff was really sweet. They decorated the staff lounge and there was a cake on one of the tables that read, "Happy Birthday, Dr. Jones." I still had a hard time hearing myself be referred to as Dr. Jones. It sounded so foreign in my ears. At one point during the day, one of the nurses pulled me aside and said, "Dr. Jones, some flowers were just delivered here for you."

"Flowers?" I smiled, thinking they were from Kendall, Kim, my parents, Ryan, or a combination of all the above. But when I went to get the flowers, which were beautiful red, long-stemmed roses in a vase with white calla lilies, there wasn't a card. I shrugged my shoulders thinking the deliveryman must have dropped it somewhere along the way.

By day's end, or should I say night's end, I showered and was getting dressed to go home when Jeanette entered the dressing room.

"Happy birthday," she said as I pulled on my sweatpants.

"Thanks."

"Have you eaten dinner?"

"I grabbed a bag of chips earlier. The emergency room was so busy tonight I never did make it down to the cafeteria."

"That's no way to spend a birthday. Give me five minutes to shower and another five to get dressed and I'll take you out for a quick bite to eat."

"Oh, Jeanette, that's sweet, but you don't have to do that. I just want to get home and go to sleep." I said as I withdrew the flowers from my locker.

"The flowers are beautiful. Viva is the best florist in the city," she said as she glanced at the flowers.

"How'd you know Viva put this arrangement together?" I asked with eyebrows raised.

"I ordered them for you."

"You did?" I asked, astonished.

"Yes."

"There wasn't a card. I'm so sorry. I didn't realize ... Thank you."

"You're welcome."

There was a weird silence as I stood there letting it sink in that the flowers were not from my girl or family, but from Jeanette, someone I barely knew.

"Will you reconsider the dinner invitation?"

"I really can't. I need to get home to *my girl*."

"Perhaps some other time?" She looked me up and down. Her penetrating stare attempted to undress me from head to toe. For the first time in my life, I understood the danger associated with strangers and locker rooms and was thankful I already had my clothes on.

"Yeah. Sure," I said as I zipped my bag and threw it over my shoulder. "Bye. Thanks again for the flowers."

"Good night, sister."

I exited the dressing room as quickly as I could. Sister? Sister my ass! Dr. Jeanette Mitchell was a lesbian. And she was diggin' on me knowing good and well that I had a girl.

"Kendall, baby, I'm on my way home to you!" I got in my car and turned the music all the way up. No amount of money would ever amount to the emotional connection Kendall and I shared.

Happy Birthday, Baby
TINA

"Surprise!" Kendall, Kim, Kwame, Miguel, and Nicole yelled as I walked into the apartment. Even little Tiara tried to yell something.

"You guys! What are you doing up this late?" I set the flowers on a table and hugged each one of them. I noticed Kendall's eyebrows raise when she saw the flowers.

"It's only eleven," Kim said.

"And it's Saturday," Kwame added.

"So what better way to spend a Saturday night is there than having a surprise birthday party with family and friends?" asked Nicole.

By this time I had reached Kendall and I walked into her arms to receive the hug and kiss I had been craving all day. Kendall did not let me down as she openly tongue-kissed me in front of everybody.

"So that's how lesbians do it, huh?" asked Nicole. "Miguel, you better act right or else I'm crossing over to the other side! That kiss looked scrumptious."

"It was," I replied as I hugged Kendall again.

"Man, those flowers are gorgeous," said Kim. "Who gave them to you?"

"Dr. Mitchell."

"Kwame, please take note, a girl wants, needs, and deserves flowers every now and then," Kim said.

"Amen to that! Miguel, you need to heed Kim's words, too," Nicole said to Miguel.

"We are not going to win this one. Let's go grab a beer," Miguel said to Kwame.

"Man, I don't even drink, but I'm right behind you." They exited the living room into safer territory.

"How was work today, baby?" Kendall asked.

"Long and busy. But the staff was great. They decorated the lounge in honor of my birthday."

"That's cool," Kim said. "And as you can see, we decorated our home in honor of your birthday. So stop all this work talk, grab a drink, eat some food." She pointed to the dining area. The table was covered with chips, pretzels, pizza, cheese cubes, grapes, and punch.

There was no delaying Miguel and Kwame who had returned from the kitchen to the dining room when they heard mention of food. Kim and Nicole followed close behind. Tiara had tuckered out during all the small talk. Kendall took my hand and held me back.

"I love you," she said as she looked directly into my eyes.

"Girl, I love you too. I've loved you for a long time. Thanks for making my birthday special."

"I have something extra special for you later on," she winked.

"How much later?"

"Bedtime later."

"I'm tired now! Let's go!"

Kendall laughed and instead of leading me to the bedroom, she led me to the table. Once there, I realized how hungry I was and loaded my plate with pizza and cheese cubes. I followed my meal with punch only to discover it was a specialty blend that included vodka. Two hours later, we were all feeling good and I was ready to get my extra special gift from Kendall.

We politely excused ourselves from the group. When we made it to the bedroom, Kendall enveloped my body with her own and then it was on. Pussy to pussy. Tongue to crotch. Diagonal. Horizontal. The legendary "X." Coochie to booty. Fingers and strap. Our lovemaking was fierce and exploratory. Satisfied and exhausted, Kendall and I fell asleep in each other's arms.

Do Unto Others
TINA

When I awoke the next morning, Kendall was still asleep in my arms, her head resting in the soft spot on my left side between my arm and my breast. Her left arm was gently draped across my stomach. And her left leg was resting on my thighs.

I inhaled the scent of her hair. It smelled like coconut oil. I caressed her back, damp from the heat generated by the closeness of our bodies. I looked over at the clock. It was just past eight. I had to be at work at one. I wanted to do something special for Kendall before I left. I decided I'd cook her breakfast – waffles with sliced strawberries and whipped cream on top, scrambled cheese eggs, sausage, and cranberry juice. I cautiously separated her body from mine. I stood, looked down at her naked body, and wished for a lifetime of happiness with her by my side.

I pulled on my robe and padded my way to the kitchen to inventory the contents of the fridge. Before I reached the kitchen, I heard Tiara stirring in her room, and went to check on her. She was sitting up in her crib playing with a stuffed animal. When she saw me, she dropped the stuffed animal, smiled, held up her arms and said, "Ti-a!"

"Hi, sweetness," I said as I reached to lift her out of the crib. "How's my girl this morning?"

Tiara mumbled something in baby talk and followed it up with a laugh. So I laughed right along with her.

"Your diaper's wet, young lady. Let's get you washed and dressed."

I took Tiara to the bathroom she and Kim shared and washed her up. I lotioned her smooth little body and sprinkled some powder on her before I put a clean diaper on her. I combed her baby-soft hair into six one-inch ponytails and chose a soft-pink Nike running suit for her attire.

"Now let's go survey the 'fridgerator. Want a bottle?"

"Ba-ble."

"Coming up," I said as I prepared Tiara's beverage. Once I got her settled, I was able to begin frying sausage for Kendall's breakfast. The whole package of sausage was simmering in the skillet when Kendall walked into the kitchen.

"Mornin', sleepy head," I said. "What are you doing up so early?"

"I thought I smelled Mama's cooking," Kendall yawned as she sat in a chair next to Tiara's high chair.

"It's not your mama's, sweetie, but it's definitely the next best thing. Want some coffee?"

"Okay. Thank you."

"Coming right up."

Kendall played quietly with Tiara for several minutes before she spoke.

"Baby, who is Dr. Mitchell?"

"She's my mentor over at the hospital."

"Why'd she give you flowers?"

"I don't know. When they were delivered, they came without a card. At first, I thought they were from you or my family and the florist dropped the card. But I learned later, from her, she was responsible. She invited me to dinner. I turned her down and came home. That's it."

"Is she a lesbian?"

"I don't know. She hasn't confided in me. I suspect she may be."

"Does she know you are?"

"Yes."

"Does she know you have a girl?"

"Yes."

"But she still sent you flowers?"

"Yes."

"And you accepted them?"

"Yes … No. I mean, yes, but I didn't know they were from her."

"When you found out who they were from, could you have given them back to her?"

"Yeah. I guess. I just didn't think it was that big of a deal."

"It is."

"Okay. I'm sorry. It won't happen again."

"Do unto others, Tina. I wouldn't do that to you. I wouldn't bring flowers home from another woman. Don't do that to me."

"Alright. I understand."

"Good. So what's for breakfast?"

"Well ... I figured all the hard work you put into my birthday present last night was deserving of a reward. So, for you, my dear, we have maple brown sugar sausage links evenly browned on all sides. Fluffy, yellow scrambled eggs with American and cheddar cheeses. Golden brown waffles – crispy – the way you like them. And topped with fresh strawberries, sliced by my own delicate hands. And a squirt or two of whipped cream! If you ask nicely, I'll also top it off with a special cream of my own," I winked. "Last, cranberry juice on ice because I know you like your juice to be ice cold." I placed the finished product in front of her.

"Wow! All this just for me?"

"Just for you, baby." I exited the kitchen to grab the flowers Dr. Mitchell had given me. I emptied the water from the vase before I slam dunked everything – vase and flowers – into the kitchen trash can.

"I love *you*, Kendall," I said again. I gently kissed her forehead and gave Tiara a high-five.

Her Word

KENDALL

If Tina gave me her word, I knew I had nothing to worry about. It was easy for me to push thoughts of Tina and Dr. Mitchell out of my mind as I surfed the internet. When I wasn't working or caring for Tiara, I tended to find myself sitting in front of the computer researching rape victims, cases, trends, and violators. It had become an obsession. I found myself thirsting for knowledge to pass on to the victims that I work with. The habit was a lot less addictive and much more informative than the chatting I used to do with strangers prior to my rape. After my rape, talking with complete strangers about myself no longer held the fascination it once did.

Tiara waddled her diapered self over to me and crawled up into my lap. I stared at my daughter and wondered how it was possible to love her as much as I did given the fact that she definitely was not created out of love. I stroked her pudgy arms and played with the little puffs of hair that Tina had so precisely sectioned off when she got Tiara dressed earlier.

My daughter. She was a deceptively wicked gift from God that I cannot imagine my life without. I prayed that I would be able to protect her from the ills of this world. Yet I wanted her to live life to the fullest and appreciate every color, smell, taste, and sound that this earth provides. I wanted to give her these things, yet shield her from these things. How was that possible?

Tiara banged on the keyboard and seemed pretty impressed with herself. My thoughts continued. A mother's love. Wow. Nothing in my life prior to Tiara had ever primed me for this moment. I didn't see how anything could ever separate a mother from the love she feels for her child. And Tiara had the love of two mothers. Tina and me. Did Tina's love go as deep as my own? Was that possible?

What would happen when Tiara grew older and realized her home is not a "normal" home as dictated by society? Would I ever be able to tell her the circumstances behind her creation? Would she ever ask me where my parents are? Would kids tease her because she has two moms? Could Tina and I instill in her the strength and power to tell outsiders to go to hell? I wondered …

My computer screen went black and Tiara looked up at me as if to say, "Wow! Did you see what I just did? How'd I do that, Mommy?"

"Look at you, Tiara. You're a genius!" I said to her as I rubbed noses with her. Tiara placed both of her pudgy hands on my cheeks and smiled at me.

"Buv boo," Tiara said, stating her version of "I love you."

"Mommy loves you too, sweetie."

Fuck Off
TINA

"Tina, how was the rest of your birthday?" Dr. Mitchell approached me as soon as I walked into the employee lounge.

"It was great."

"Wonderful." She had a way of drawing out her *Rs* that really irked me. "How about that dinner tonight?"

"I don't think so," I said while thinking to myself that this lady was starting to piss me off.

Dr. Mitchell stepped closer to me. I backed away because I hate for people to be in my personal space.

"You couldn't possibly still be celebrating your birthday this evening," she said as she rubbed a pointed, expensively manicured fingertip down my arm. The touch was meant to be provocative, I'm sure.

"Look, I've thanked you for the flowers. You really didn't have to do that. I'm not interested in having dinner with you. Not today. Not tomorrow. Nor the next day. I'm finding the manner that you're stepping to me to be extremely offensive and I would really appreciate it if you would just back the fuck off!" The words were out of my mouth before I had a chance to fully think about the impact they would make. Too late to swallow my words, I stood my ground and waited for Dr. Mitchell's reaction.

She arched her eyebrows before she squinted her heavily mascaraed eyes. "How unfortunate. You just turned down the opportunity of a lifetime. With my power, money, and endorsement, you could have been the next black female force in this city. Below me, of course. By giving me a little taste of you, you could have gone a long, long way. Now, my sister, you're on your own."

Not to appear defeated, I said, "I'm not for sale. No one gets a taste of me except my girl. I don't give a damn how much money and clout you have." I was sweating profusely under my arms, but I played it like a pro and kept my arms to my side so she wouldn't notice.

"So naïve. Once you hit the struggle, sister, you'll come running."

"When I hit the struggle, I'll run straight to my girl – not to some old-ass, frustrated, plugged-up bitch like you!"

"Whatever, Dr. Jones. Don't bother discussing this with anyone. No one would ever believe you." She whisked away, white doctor's coat flapping behind her closeted rich ass.

That's My Girl

KENDALL

When Tina called and told me about her encounter with Dr. Mitchell, I couldn't believe it. What an arrogant bitch! My girl managed to handle her business. I was proud of Tina. She's always been able to step out on faith and stand up for what she believes in. I prayed, though, that her tongue-lashing hadn't landed her in a career sinkhole.

"Yo Kendall, it's almost time for the game. Cleveland and San Francisco. Who ya got?" Kwame's question interrupted my thoughts. I watched him head towards the kitchen to undoubtedly grab some snacks.

"I gotta cheer on my team. Cleveland all the way!" I said.

"Thank you, Kendall! I keep trying to tell Kwame that San Francisco can't take Cleveland." Kim smiled.

"Whatever! When was the last time you saw Cleveland in the playoffs?" asked Kwame.

"When was the last time you saw San Francisco in the playoffs? It damn sure hasn't been in your lifetime!" Kim retaliated.

"You're right. I haven't seen them get there. Yet. But I know they've seen the glare of the ring more recently than Cleveland! What the hell does their team name mean anyway?" Kwame joked.

"Yo. Yo. Y'all ready to watch this game?" Miguel asked as he and Nicole bounded through the front door arms full with grocery sacks.

"What's up, man? Miguel, I was just telling these ladies – Cleveland fans – that they can't take San Francisco."

Miguel laughed. "Quiet as it's kept, man, neither one of these teams deserves bragging rights. Now you want to talk football, I gotta give a plug to Tampa Bay. It's all about the Bay, baby!"

"Miguel, please. Aren't you from Miami? Why aren't you plugging your home team?" Kim asked.

"'Cause Miami is just as bad as San Francisco and Cleveland," Nicole answered for him.

"I got relatives in Tampa," Miguel said as he tried to justify why he wasn't rooting for his home team.

"Baby, I love you, but I can't stand here and let you lie. You know good and well you don't have no family in Tampa!" Nicole laughed.

"I do. They distant cousins on my father's mother's sister's side." Miguel grinned sheepishly.

"Whatever, man. You want a drink?" Kwame asked.

"For real, I do. They're distant cousins," Miguel said as he followed Kwame into the kitchen.

"Y'all can take these groceries in there!" Nicole yelled after them as she sat in the recliner. "This has been a fantastic weekend. I'm going to hate going to work tomorrow."

"Right," I said. "My parents use to tell me all the time that being grown ain't as much fun as it sounds."

"Thank God I'm not fully grown," Kim giggled.

At that point, the fellas brought bags of chips into the living room and laid them on the table. They went back to get the drinks. Tiara played quietly on the floor in the space between the tv and the table. The rest of us sat on the couch and chairs and munched on chips as the game started.

At half-time, Cleveland was up seventeen to ten. Kim and Kwame were in the middle of a friendly shouting match as Kim took bragging rights for the half-time victory. Kwame quickly responded that the game wasn't over yet. Nicole and Miguel interjected their comments just to instigate and add fuel to the already heated fire. Tiara had teetered out midway into the second quarter so I scooped her up and took her to her room where I would lay her down for the night.

No

TINA

I unlocked the door and walked into the apartment just as Kendall scooped Tiara up from the floor. I went over to them and placed a petal-soft kiss on Tiara's forehead and winked at Kendall as they left the room. Then I plopped down in the spot where Kendall must have been sitting as they all watched the game.

Everyone said hi to me as I walked in, but I was pretty much ignored as Kim and Kwame lovingly argued about the game they had been watching and Nicole and Miguel went to the kitchen to get drink refills. I was silently grateful for the opportunity to melt into the deep crevices of the tan couch. What a day!

My eyes were about to close as I reflected on the day's events, but then I heard the announcer say, "Tonio Thompson is having a subpar game …" My eyes opened to looked at the picture of Tonio and his stats for the season.

There was something familiar about Tonio's face. Of course he looked familiar; I knew him, he was my ex. But I hadn't seen Tonio since I ran into him when he was in Atlanta doing volunteer work. Yet, it seemed like I had just seen him. I stared at his face and tuned the announcers out. Then I focused on his mole. He has a mole right above his lip on the left side of his face. Slowly, I sat up from the couch. I leaned forward and stared at his picture. My stomach felt queasy. Tight. I raised my eyes from his picture displayed on the television set and looked upward at the eight-by-ten of Tiara that was sitting atop the television. I looked at the small mole right above her lip on the left side of her face. I looked at her mouth, her nose, back to the mole. Then I looked at her eyes in the picture and back down to the screen where Tonio's piercing gaze met all who dared to look at him. I felt my stomach sink as Tonio's picture faded away and I realized that Tonio and Tiara share a striking, haunting resemblance.

I'll Be Your Strength
KENDALL

Later that evening, after Cleveland's victory, Tina and I lay in bed holding one another. Tina had been quiet all evening. She was distant. Very little laughter came from her usually bubbly self.

"Baby, what is it?" I asked as I gently rubbed her shoulder.

"Nothing. I'm just tired. I can't keep up with you party animals."

"Turn over. Let me give you a massage."

Tina gladly turned over. She used both her arms to tuck her pillow under her face. I straddled her firm, round ass and felt myself become aroused as I slowly kneaded the knots from her neck, shoulders, and back. Tina lay there quietly as I worked. Her green eyes stared at the wall and I knew something was on her mind. What was it?

I bent to kiss her shoulder blades and let my fingertips walk gently along her side. She squirmed a little bit. Ticklish. Then I let my hand glide across her lower back as I scooted down her body and let my lips kiss that small nook where back meets bottom. My hands gripped her waist as I continued to kiss and lick her lower back and attempted to bring her thoughts to me.

She stirred a little. My tongue slowly traveled down the place where both sides of her curvaceous ass meet. Tina turned over and I found myself face to face with her well-lined and lightly shaved pubic region. I could smell a combination of her moisture and cinnamon spice shower gel. I kissed her hood and sucked her clit.

I felt Tina's hands on my shoulders. She massaged them briefly. Then she put her hand under my chin and raised my face so that our eyes met. She looked right through me as I raised my body and inched upwards so that our faces were mere inches apart.

"What's wrong, Tina?"

She just shook her head from left to right. No words. A single tear fell from the corner of her left eye. I kissed it away. Then she hugged me close and I could feel her body tremble underneath my own.

I no longer probed her for answers. As my baby's body shook beneath me, I felt engulfed by her fears. The strength that I'd always been able to find within Tina seemed to melt away like butter being spread on a piece of fresh, hot toast. I'd never known Tina to be vulnerable, but here, tonight, I knew that she was. And then, because I loved her more than I loved myself, I held her and allowed her to melt safely as I shielded her from whatever had caused her to break.

The Investigation Begins
TINA

I heard Tiara crying early Monday morning. I tried to ease myself up and out of the bed, but I felt weighted down by the realization that Tonio may have brought harm to Kendall and her family.

I felt Kendall shift beside me. She kissed my cheek and glanced into my eyes. She stroked my face and rose up to throw on a t-shirt and shorts before she went to tend to Tiara.

I watched her retreating figure as she opened our bedroom door and closed it behind her. I stared at the closed door and no longer heard Tiara whimpering which meant that Kendall had reached her. My mind was racing as I considered the possibility that Tonio had raped Kendall, murdered her parents, and fathered Tiara.

The Tonio I knew and had once loved was not that kind of man. He was a gentle teddy bear. Yet the resemblance between him and Tiara was uncanny. Why hadn't I noticed it before?

Why would Tonio do this? How could he? Was this my fault? When I ran into him at the children's clinic he mentioned he knew I had a relationship with Kendall. Did he blame her for our break up? Did he harm her to get back at me?

The questions popped into my head nonstop. I was thankful that I was off today. After Kendall and Kim left, I needed to do some investigating of my own. If my suspicions were right, Tonio Thompson was a murderer, rapist, and father.

How Can I Help You?
KENDALL

This morning wasn't much better than last night. Tina was still distant. She didn't even get out of bed this morning before I left. That's not like Tina. She's the morning person!

Tina's body finally stopped trembling last night when she drifted off to sleep. But she didn't sleep well. I watched her for a long time. She tossed. And turned. And moaned.

Was she dreaming about the situation with Dr. Mitchell? Had something more happened that she hadn't told me about? Was her job in jeopardy?

Thoughts of Tina were sidelined as I entered my workplace and was approached by a young girl. She couldn't have been more than fifteen.

"Can you help me, please? I'm trying to find room B34 so I can take drum therapy with my girlfriend."

"Um … sure. B34 is down the hall. First left."

"Thank you." She began to saunter away.

I called after her. "Excuse me …" I paused because I didn't know her name.

"Janay. My name is Janay."

"Okay, Janay. My name is Kendall. Did you say your girlfriend?" I probed.

Janay immediately took the defensive. "Yes, I said girlfriend." She rolled her eyes.

"No. No. Don't get angry. I didn't mean it like that. I'm family," I said using the identifier that gay people often use to refer to each other.

The girl, Janay, relaxed a little. Then she said, "What business is it of yours anyway?"

"None," I said. "I just really like the idea of you supporting your girlfriend by attending drum therapy with her. I used drum therapy during my own recovery."

"Recovery from what?"

"Rape."

"Yeah, well my girl's family kicked her out when they found out she liked girls instead of boys. She had no place to go. She was living on the streets. Do you know how many teenagers turn to the streets for shelter because their families are tripping about something? Do you know how many teens flee their households because they're being abused and fucked with? Kids are screwed up because adults never get their own issues worked out. They just carry their shit and dump it on their kids. How do y'all expect us to cope when y'all never handled your own issues?

"My girl had to rely on the streets, but even the streets can turn wicked. She was raped by a group of dumb-ass boys who shouldn't have been out runnin' the streets! I wasn't there to protect my girl. This drum therapy is just as much for me as it is for her."

I could tell Janay wanted and needed to talk. In those brief moments, she had laid out more truths than any doctor ever had. I wanted to be the person to listen to her. I reached into my purse and pulled out my business card. "Call me," I said. "We have a lot in common."

Janay snatched the card from my hand, read it, and jammed it into her pocket as she hurried to room B34.

I walked into my office. I turned the lights on, sat at my desk, and flipped on the computer. I leaned back in my chair and reflected on my own drum therapy lessons.

Drum therapy was a fairly new phenomenon in the world of psychiatric treatment. While I didn't know its origins, my counselor had enrolled me in a course as part of my treatment following the rape. The therapy allowed me to express my anger in a nonviolent manner. Beating on that drum helped me to non-verbally express myself when the words simply wouldn't come. Drumming was a great way for me to pour my emotions out. I hoped Janay and her girlfriend could both heal with the power of drumming.

The hotline telephone rang.

"You've reached the crisis center. This is a safe and secure hotline. How can I help you?" I asked as memories of my own healing were pushed into the same place where I temporarily stored Tina's situation and attempted to help the distressed caller.

Murderer

TINA

It was just as I suspected. My search on the internet revealed that Tonio's team was in town the weekend of the murder and rape. But the game took place on a Sunday night. The rape took place late Friday afternoon. Tonio's team wouldn't have been there that Friday. But would Tonio?

I sighed and took a sip of coffee. Should I call the investigator and reveal my suspicions? What if I was wrong? I didn't really have any proof. Tiara and Tonio just looked alike. Big deal.

If I was right, bringing my suspicions to light could uncover a murderer. If Tonio was guilty, Kendall's parents could finally rest in peace. Kendall could be at ease.

I rolled my head around in a circle and attempted to pop the bones in my neck. I tapped my pen on my coffee mug. I picked up the phone.

A moment or two passed before I heard, "Police department. How can I help you?"

"I need to speak to Detective Radcliff. It's an emergency."

Society
KENDALL

I stepped out of my office for my lunch break and heard someone crying in the hallway. I walked towards the crying. I rounded the corner and saw the young teenager, Janay, and another girl that I assumed was her girlfriend.

"I'm so sorry, Michelle. I should have been there for you," Janay said between her sobs.

Michelle, who was smaller than Janay, didn't say anything. I watched them hold on to one another as they tried to absorb energy, strength, and perseverance to carry on. For Michelle, it was the energy to keep living. To go on with her life and leave the rape in the past which is a very difficult feat to accomplish. For Janay, it was the strength to be there for her girl even though she had not been there to protect her from the monstrous and hateful act of rape. For both of them, it was the perseverance to continue forward in a lifestyle that so many people deem ungodly and unnatural.

I thought back to Tina's and my relationship in high school. All of the elements were there for our relationship back then. Tina knew she was a lesbian, but she didn't know how to come out. I didn't know I was gay until Tina entered my life. Some people would think that I became gay after I was raped. That's not true. The rape did not turn me into a lesbian. Loving Tina did.

Society had somehow taken it upon itself to be the judge here on earth. Society dictated what was acceptable and unacceptable. What gave society the right? People want to holler about it being a choice and how gayness can be corrected, but both instances are not true. Being homosexual was not a choice.

The only choice I and others like me have is that of do I like thick girls or thin, short or tall, brown eyes or blue, smart or dumb, giggly or serious. Go down the line! Those are the only choices of concern when it comes to being a homosexual. The choices aren't any different than those of a straight person.

My gayness can't be fixed! It can be denied. Hell, I've done that for years. All my denial did was make me depressed and lonely. Why should I live my life sad and in solitude? And what the hell gives society the right to try and make me deny myself?

Then there's the Bible. Dammit. I am a Christian woman and I believe in God. I was brought up in the church and I believe in heaven and hell. I talk to God daily and He guides me in the choices I make. I'm going to heaven because sin I have not! Love, I have. And love, I will. One woman. For the rest of my life.

Refocusing on the two girls in front of me, I silently backed away and allowed them the space they needed to connect and heal.

"You go, girls." I whispered to myself. "Dare to be different. Live your lives with love for one another and God in your hearts. Don't let society be your judge. Life is too short to deny yourselves inner peace and happiness."

I only wish I had done it sooner.

Baby, Let's Talk
TINA

Once I placed the call to Detective Radcliff and voiced my suspicions, things happened quickly. He kept me in the loop as the mystery unraveled. Flight records verified Tonio had flown into town Friday morning. He flew in separately from the team. They didn't arrive until Saturday evening. A rental car search revealed he had rented a car for one day, Friday only. Hotel records showed he stayed at a downtown hotel under a false name, but using his own credit card on Friday, and with his team at a different hotel on Saturday. Conversations with coaches revealed he did not practice with the team on Friday, which we knew since his flight records had been seized and shown that he was already in town. He was fined by the team and rode the bench during the Sunday game. But the clincher, the evidence that prompted the detectives to bring him in for questioning, was his shoe size. Tonio's shoe size, fifteen, was the same size as the print authorities measured in the grass outside of Kendall's home.

"Tina, this is Detective Radcliff," I heard as I placed my cell phone to my ear.

"Yes, detective."

"I want you to know that we have the suspect, Tonio Thompson, in our custody for questioning in the murder of Mr. and Mrs. Long and the rape of Kendall Long. With the help of San Francisco authorities, we are also, simultaneously, conducting a search at the suspect's home. Would you like to share the news with Kendall or would you prefer that I do it? Either way, we'd like for her to come home as soon as possible."

My hands felt clammy and I felt moisture dripping under my arms as I answered, "Let me tell her, detective."

I don't know why my head started to ache as I contemplated how to tell Kendall that Tonio may have been responsible for her parents' death. Unfortunately, I didn't have much time to consider the best approach because Kendall came through the front door.

"Hey, baby," she said as she walked in and gave me a hug.

"Hey, yourself," I replied. "How was work?"

"It was good."

"Kendall, let's talk," I said not wanting to prolong the conversation. I took Kendall by the hand and led her to the couch.

"Tina, what's wrong?"

"Well ... Does Tiara look like anyone you know?"

"Huh? She looks like my baby."

"I know. I mean ... does she resemble anybody from your, our past?"

Kendall looked at Tiara's picture for a moment. "No."

"Wait here." I rose up and went to the bedroom to get my laptop. I brought the computer to the couch and keyed in some information. "Now look," I said turning the screen towards Kendall. Tonio's football picture was displayed.

Kendall exhaled and began to shake. "No way! No fucking way!"

"It's not certain, Kendall. Detective Radcliff has done some investigating. Tonio was in town that weekend. He wears the same size shoe as the perpetrator." I swear I could see the veins pulsing in Kendall's neck.

"How long have you known this?"

"First of all, I don't know anything. But I got a hunch the night of the San Francisco and Cleveland game. The network showed an image of Tonio and the resemblance to Tiara was incredible. Especially the mole."

"So this is why you've been acting so strange for the past few days?"

"Yes."

"Jesus."

"Detective Radcliff wants you to go home. Authorities in California are searching Tonio's home. They already have Tonio in for questioning."

"Well ... I guess I better pack my bags and catch the next plane."

"Not without me." I lowered my head and placed my forehead against Kendall's.

Waiting
KENDALL

By the time Tina and I had called to reserve seats for a flight, packed our bags, and headed to the airport, the media had gotten wind of Tonio's possible involvement. Needless to say, they were having a field day with the possibility of a pro football player committing murder and rape.

When the plane touched down, Tina and I made a quiet trek to the police station. Outside the station, reporters lurked and waited for news on Tonio.

"Kendall. Tina. Pleasure to see you both. Come in here where it's quiet." Detective Radcliff led us to an office.

"I have some developments for you. First, we've taken a semen sample from Tonio. If it doesn't match the semen we collected at the scene, we're back to square one. If it does match, we have solved this case."

"Oh my God," Kendall said.

"Kendall, how do you know Tonio?" Detective Radcliff asked.

"He was Tina's boyfriend. She dated him before we became lovers."

Detective Radcliff massaged his temples. "So this is a case of a lover scorned? Tonio was jealous and heartbroken over losing Tina. He seeks vengeance. Commits murder. Rapes you. Vindication."

There was a knock on the door and Detective Radcliff excused himself as he went out to talk to his colleague. Tina and I watched as the officers conversed outside the door. Detective Radcliff quickly came back into his office.

"The search of Tonio Thompson's home revealed a folder, Kendall, with your personal e-mail address, home address, driving directions from the airport to your parents' house, and your photo with an *X* on your face. We now have probable cause and we'll arrest him. Lucky for us, when we asked for a semen sample, he did not request a lawyer or deny us the sample. All we need is the DNA test to come back as a match. Kendall, is there anything else about the evening that you can remember?"

"No."

"Okay. Why don't you ladies wait here until the tests are finished?"

Time seemed to stand still as Tina and I waited for the tests to come back. So many questions pulsed through my mind. The biggest question, though, was why?

"The tests are conclusive. Hair and semen samples collected at the scene of the crime match those that we took from Tonio a little while ago. It's over, ladies. Tonio Thompson is being booked for murder and rape. It's over."

You Lied

TINA

To ease my mind, I went to visit Tonio. As I looked at him through the glass partition, it was easy to see that he was not the man I once loved. He looked mean and hardened. As he sat and picked up the phone to speak to me, his gaze was accusatory. And while no words had yet been spoken between us, I instantly knew that he blamed me as the stimuli that caused his psychological metamorphosis and spiral downward.

"What are you doing here?" he said into the phone.

"I came to look you in the eye and ask you why you did this."

"Why?" he repeated back to me. "You sit there with your prim and proper ass and ask me why? You left me for a woman, Tina. We were together for three beautiful years and you ask me why? You exchanged my dick for her pussy! You humiliated me and you sit there and ask me why!"

"Tonio ..."

"Tonio, nothing! From what I understand, you don't just wake up one morning and decide I think I'll be gay today! Folks like you claim they know from jump. So tell me, why the hell did you date me?"

I thought for a moment before I answered. "You know what, Tonio, you're right. I've known I like women since I was a kid. But our society doesn't like folks like me. So I tried to become someone that society would like. I tried to love men. I tried to like intercourse with men. You. But no matter how hard I tried, I couldn't. I prayed to be regular. Honest, I did. Yet, I never felt like I could soar when I was with you. I felt like I was settling. When this thing happened between me and Kendall, I finally felt at ease. Everything felt right. Finally."

"Well, I'm glad your life finally felt right 'cause mine went to hell. I loved you. You screwed me. I can explain the rape. Shit. I just wanted to find out what was so good about her pussy to make you want to leave me. I can't explain the parents. Rage, I guess. Call it fuckin' rage."

"Let me get this straight. My leaving you made you so mad that you up and killed somebody? I don't think so. I'll admit, I was wrong for living my life as a lie and not coming out sooner. I take full responsibility for that and I'd change it in a heartbeat if I could. But that's all I did wrong. My relationship with you was not a lie. When I made love to you, I was loving you and only you. Our love was not a lie and I'm not going to sit here and allow you to claim that it was. Hear me when I say, I loved you, Tonio. But I fell in love with someone else. Loving somebody and being in love with someone are two different things. I fell in love with a woman. If it had been a man, would you have run off and killed his parents and raped him? Would it have been more respectable for you to lose me to a guy? What kind of macho bullshit is that? You need to decide if you're mad that I left you or if you're mad that I left you for a woman. And no matter which one you choose, it still doesn't justify murder or rape, you asshole!"

"I don't need to decide shit. I'm mad about the whole situation. You and your lesbian sisterhood need to stop playing with the male mind."

"That's where you're wrong. I didn't play with your mind. I didn't string you along or step out on you. I kept it real and told you I was done with our relationship. It's not my fault that your microscopic male mind couldn't accept that!"

"This is your fault, Tina. I don't give a damn how you present your side of the story. You lied to yourself and you lied to me."

"Whatever, Tonio. But only you committed murder and rape. And now, you're going to spend the rest of your life in a cell. You extinguished two, happy lives. And you temporarily dimmed the spirit of a third life. The ironic thing though is that you also gave life. And now, the two women you despise most are loving, nurturing, and teaching your very own. How's that for a twist of fate?"

Tonio put the phone down and leaned back in his chair with his jaw hung low. I can't begin to pretend to know what was running through his mind. But as I pushed my chair back and rose to walk away, the one thing I knew for certain was I felt guilty. If I had been true to myself about my sexuality sooner, I probably never would've dated him. Then maybe this never would have happened.

The Beat of Our Own Drum

KENDALL

Tina and I entered room B34 hand-in-hand. The room was set in a circle with chairs placed around the border. As students filed into the room, they each picked up a drum and found a chair to sit in. Tina and I followed suit. Sitting next to each other, across the circle from us, were Janay and Michelle.

There was no talking as the instructor tapped a soft beat on her drum. The class immediately followed; each person began to beat her own drum. The only thing that could be heard was the tap tap tapping of the sheepskin. At first, all the drums were in sync. Then a haggard pounding broke away from the rhythm of the rest of the group. I looked over at Tina and discovered that it was she who had let her emotions break free. Soon, others followed suit. No longer synchronized, the drumming in the room became angry. Cries could be heard via the pounding of the drums. This mass chaos continued for ten, maybe fifteen minutes before each individual became tired and weary after releasing her own inner turmoil.

SHE *Slipped* AND FELL

I watched Tina as she tried to catch her breath. I know she feels responsible for Tonio's demise. But it's not her fault. She is not guilty. I will not allow her to believe that she is.

The evening Tina and I innocently slipped and fell changed our lives. The fall was much more than a physical act. It was an awakening in the sexual, moral, and psychological senses too. And even though others were indirectly affected by our fall, no one has been more affected by it than we were. And no one should be allowed to blame us for his own inner battles.

So Tina and I are taking this drumming class and we're going to counseling, too. Through it we seek tolerance for those things we cannot change. We seek forgiveness for those we have hurt and those who have hurt us. But most importantly, we will find acceptance for who we are and who we love. And when it's all said and done, we will encourage others like us to just be.